THE PLEASURE EXPERIMENT

BARBARA CONNELL

Contents

1

CHAPTER 1

S asha POV

"Are you crazy!?" My best friend, Jenna Stone, shouted in my face.

"No. I'm perfectly sane. I mean it too, I'm not backing out of this." I retorted calmly as I unwrapped another chocolate and popped the delicious smooth dessert into my mouth.

"Sasha, be serious. You can't just think that all men will cheat or leave you. Yeah, there are some real scum bags out there but majority of guys aren't. Take my brother for example, he's a great guy. Sure I hear a little too much info from the tabloids sometimes but he's never been one to cheat or anything."

"That's because he does exactly what I intend to do! Jenna... listen, I'm 24 years old and every single guy I've dated has been a lying cheating prick who couldn't keep his fucking dick in his pants. I want a loyal husband and children one day and how can I have that if the guy I date has wondering eyes?"

"So, instead of dating or even staying single until the right guy come along like a normal woman you plan on doing a 'sexual experiment'?!" She cried using her fingers to quote 'sexual experiment'.

I sighed. I knew I should have thought twice about telling Jenna. I'd been thinking about this idea for a while now. Ever since my latest heart break cheated on me I decided enough was enough. It was obvious that I wasn't good enough at sex and that was why every guy I dated cheated on me.

After I kicked his sorry ass out of my apartment I started sorting all my research on sex, foreplay, toys, role playing, fantasies and how to pleasure a man and compiled them into a survey. I was going to take notes and pretty much turn everything into a detailed document on how to keep my future husband interested in me.

I looked at Jenna and pulled out my deadly weapon, the puppy dog eyes.

"Oh Jesus... Stop! Stop! Sasha for the love of God, FINE! But at least keep to one guy instead of sleeping with a bunch of different guys. It'll at least be safer for you."

"But how will the survey work if it's done with one... ok! Fine!" I stopped half way through my sentence because Jenna pulled out her deadly weapon, the evil glare. "Well, then the only question is... who's the lucky guy?"

"My brother of course."

I choked on the delicious goodness of melting chocolate and felt my eyes water. Her brother?! Jacob! Jacob was her fraternal twin. Deliciously tasty and oh so forbidden.

I gasped for air while Jenna thudded my back. Finally I breathed in fresh beautiful oxygen and turned to my psychotic best friend.

"Jacob? As in Jacob Stone, your twin? As in my boss!!" I cried, staring at her incredulously.

"Yep! What? He's single now, and it looks like for good, thank God! He finally dumped that cow and it looks like he's really had enough."

Jacob had dated his, now, ex-girlfriend Ava Thomas on and off for two years. She was a bikini model and had the body to die for, and she knew it.

"No Jen, I can't. Firstly he's your brother, that's totally off-limits, plus he's my boss! Completely forbidden fruit!" I sighed, yes he was my boss. I was secretary to Jacob Stone, CEO to the billion dollar shipping company, and I'd had more than my share of dirty dreams of him.

"Who's forbidden fruit?" A deep masculine voice echoed through the room. We both jumped at the intrusion and sat up from Jenna's bed to see Jacob leaning against the frame of her doorway crossing a leg over the over.

He was pure male, jet black hair cut into a neat business style, chocolate brown eyes that could melt your insides or freeze your soul. He had strong and chiselled features, including his body, and no matter what he wore his perfect abs were always obvious. He had strong shoulders which narrowed to a tight butt and strong powerful legs.

He was smirking at us with an eyebrow raised waiting for an answer. Before I could tell Jenna not to say anything she went ahead and blurted everything I had just told her.

By the time she finished explaining, my mouth had dropped open to an unattractive 'O' and I was giving Jenna the biggest death glares of her life.

"So, what I think would be a great idea is if YOU were the guy she experimented on. Obviously you're the first guy to trust and know that she'd be safe with and if you start to not be into it then you'd straight up tell her, instead of cheating on her like her bastard of an ex-boyfriend."

Jacob stared blankly at Jenna the entire time with a small furrowed expression. When she finally let the opportunity hanging in the air his eyes slid over to me. His chocolate gaze held mine before sliding to my lips then my neck, they gazed on my full cleavage before rolling over my waist and hips and trailed along my legs and feet. By the time they reached back up to my eyes I felt as though he had completely undressed me and had me naked in front of him.

"I don't know, ladies. There's a lot of things to consider, the most important being that I'm her boss."

I sighed, I didn't actually realise I was hoping for him to say yes until disappointed and rejection surged through me. Of course he'd say no.

Feeling embarrassed all of a sudden, I shot up and mumbled a hasty goodbye to Jenna and Jacob before slipping my black ballet flats on and my black coat over my red mini dress.

"I'll call you later, Jen." I murmured before dashing out of her room and towards their front door.

Just as I reached out for the door knob, a strong hand grabbed mine and turned me around pushing my back into the door.

Jacob's brown eyes were so close, oh so close, and he pressed his hard body against mine making me whimper. He traced his nose along my jaw and brought his lips to my ear lobe biting it gently.

"I never said 'no' Sasha." He whispered to me, before placing a feather light kiss on the corner of my mouth. His arousal was apparent through his jeans, and he grinded it against my mound pulling my dress up slightly. "I'll see you tomorrow at work."

Then all of a sudden, he was gone. I was left panting, heart racing and wet against a door. Oh God, I hope he says 'yes'!

I walked out of the elevator at work and headed towards the kitchen to make Jacob his morning coffee. I glanced at my reflection in the mirror that was, for some particular reason, in the kitchen. I'd dressed in my usual crisp white business shirt with tailored black blazer over the top and matching black business skirt that ended at mid thigh.

Since I was tall I never wore heels much and usually kept to my ballet flats. My dark brown hair was up in its normal bun and my black square glasses framed my emerald green eyes. I only wore a little mascara and a nude lipstick and slapped my cheeks for colour instead of wearing blush.

I looked at the clock, 8:58am, Jacob should be in his office in exactly two minutes. I walked towards his office and just as I placed his coffee down on his mahogany desk his door opened and he walked in his navy blue suit.

"Good morning, Jacob. You need to check your emails and I've already placed your important letters in your inbox. You have a meeting with Mr Lee and some of his clients at 3pm but otherwise you're completely free. Was there anything else?" I stated. I liked to come in earlier than what was actually expected just so I could be up to speed by the time he arrived.

"Thanks Sasha, and no that should be all for now." I nodded and turned to go back to my office which was just outside his. Like his office mine had glass walls and wooden blinds in case I wanted privacy.

"Oh actually..." I heard him say, I turned around and waited patiently. "About yesterday Sasha"

My face reddened and my eyes widened.

"Oh! God... Jacob, I'm so sorry you had to hear about that. It's so embarrassing! It's ok, I know you're going to say no but that's totally understandable and completely reasonable. I mean-..."

"Actually, I was going to say yes, I'll help you with your little... experiment." His breath tickled my face as he looked down at me. Whoa, when did he get so close! "You are so beautiful Sasha. It completely baffles me how anyone can cheat on someone like you"

All of a sudden his lips came crashing down on mine. Oh my God. His lips were soft but firm, and he tasted like coffee. His hands found their way to my lower back and he pulled me to him crushing my body against his hard abs and chest.

He licked my bottom lip and I opened to him. His tongue caressed mine and they did an intimate tango. I wound my arms around his neck and buried my hands into his soft hair. Mmm, just the right length to pull but not too long.

Thank God his blinds were shut!

"Mmm, Jacob" I moaned against his tantalising lips. His hands cupped my ass and lifted me up as though I weighed nothing and instantly my legs tied themselves around his waist. His erection was straining against his pants and pushing towards my core. He walked up to the door and locked it before going back and sitting me on his desk.

I grounded against him, I just couldn't get enough. Somehow every single touch from Jacob sent little electric shocks through my body. I swept his desk free of work laid down holding his lustful gaze. He leant over me and began kissing and sucking my neck, I felt his fingers unbuttoning my blouse and gasped when the cool air hit my heated skin.

I lifted his head and he stared at my body. I felt completely wanton with my blazer falling off my shoulder and my blouse undone keeping my black lace bra on display and my skirt bunched up to my waist.

"Beautiful." Jacob growled before dipping his head over a hard nipple and biting it through the lace. He grabbed the front of my bra and pulled the cups down allowing my breasts to spill into his open hands. He kneaded, plucked, sucked, licked and bit my nipples causing waves and waves of pleasure to take over.

I raised my hand and began rubbing him through his pants and felt his become impossibly harder. He groaned and bit my breast sucking hard while thrusting against my hand. Almost as though he lost all control he grabbed my bare legs and pulled me towards him and tore off my blazer along with my blouse. He pulled my skirt up and ripped my lace thong off in one swoop.

He kneeled down and spread my legs resting them on his shoulders. I didn't know what he was doing until I felt his mouth hone straight onto my pussy. I screamed into my hand and began gasping and moaning. There was nothing slow about him as he lick and sucked my clit. He moaned and the vibrations sent my body on overdrive! I was in heaven as he devoured my intimate most part.

He inserted a finger while continuing to lick my pussy then added another. Jacob was stroking me faster and faster while licking my juices as though he just emerged from the desert. I could feel my orgasm building rapidly, my channel squeezed his fingers as he continued to stroke my g-spot. I screamed his name while biting my fist to muffle the sound.

I was coming down from cloud nine when I heard a metallic zip. I looked towards him and smirked, my turn. I slid off the desk and before he could stop me I held his erection in my grasp. He was huge! I moaned, oh hell yeah he was going to feel so amazing inside me.

I began to pump him and looked up at him. I held his gaze as I slowly licked the head of his erection with my tongue, swirling it around the tip and closing my mouth over it to suck gently. I found the little ridge at the bottom of the tip and slid my tongue over it over and over and saw his eyes roll to the back of his head.

"Oh fuck Sasha!" He moaned and grabbed the edge of the desk to steady himself

I took his whole length into my mouth over and over, feeling it hit the back of my throat while I followed with my hand and the other caressed his balls.

I sucked his erection and licked from the bottom of his balls all the way up his shaft and dipped my head over his tip while furiously stroking his shaft.

"Fuck! Oh God Sasha!" He cried. He lifted me up and flipped me to my stomach on the desk and leant over me.

"I'm going to fuck you Sasha, hard and fast until you scream my name like a curse word." Before I could moan he entered me fast, his hands like twin vices on my hips as he pumped into me. He was entering so deep and hitting the hilt every time that I didn't know when I started and he ended.

I was gasping with every thrust, my hot hard nipples rubbing against the cold desk, I could feel my pussy tightening around his hard cock, grabbing at him until I exploded with pleasure. I screamed his name like he said I would into my hand and felt his thrust twice more before his fingers dug into my hips and he cried out my name in pleasure and collapsed on top of me.

The pleasure had been so intense I'm surprised I didn't black out. I felt him kissing down my spine, sending shivers all over my already sensitive body.

"Fucking hell Sasha, you nearly killed me sucking me off like that. That was amazing." He panted.

I smiled at that and could feel him starting to harden again. God he must be a machine! He chuckled and pulled out of me slowly making me groan at the sensation but feeling empty.

"You're so tight, you feel absolutely wonderful."

"Jacob..." Oh wow, I could speak? "That was just... wow." I stared into his dilated pupils and saw that he loved it just as much as I did. I sighed, "Why don't we finish this later, we have work to do now and I'm surprised no one came to check whether or not I'm dying with all the screaming you made me do" I smirked at him.

He chuckled a sexy chuckle and nodded. "You're right, as always."

I fixed myself up, as did he, and then from the corner of my eye I spotted something and grinned. I walked over to the window and grabbed my ripped thong, I walked up to him and tucked it into his back pocket grabbing his deliciously tight ass.

"I guess I won't be needing that then." Then with a parting glance I left the room and the sex god that stood staring after me.

2

CHAPTER 2

Jacob's POV

Holy damn what the hell just happened?

The question had been pounding through my head ever since I watched Sasha's sexy ass sway out of my office. I always found her intriguing and beautiful but I never looked at her in a sexual partner kind of way due to her friendship with my twin.

It was odd to think that Jenna was the one pushing for us to sleep together. But at the moment I couldn't thank her enough. Note to self, buy Jenna a huge Christmas present!

I noticed that I was still standing up staring at my door and quickly sat at my desk before someone noticed me acting like an idiot. I went through my emails and replied to whatever needed to be dealt with urgently. Thankfully there wasn't much paperwork today so I started on them. All of a sudden a thought hit me and I quickly walked over to Sasha's office.

She had an adjoining door to my office as well as another door that opened to the rest of the outside office so I used the adjoining one. I peeked in and saw that she'd taken off her blazer and had a few buttons undone, oh wait no, those button were missing from our little escapade.

I grinned and noticed her cleavage swell up everytime she took a breath and I felt my mouth watering. Fuck, get a hold on yourself Jacob! You're acting a randy teenager! Just as I was about to speak she closed her eyes and leaned back stretching her arms above her head. Her breasts perked up higher and her neck was oh so exposed that I felt myself harden at the sight.

"Well isn't that a sight to see." I said trying to sound casual. She turned and grinned shaking her head.

"You haven't seen anything yet," I heard her say, "What can I help you with Jake?"

"Oh so many things Sasha, if what we did earlier was anything to say the least. But for now I needed to ask you a question." She quirked an eyebrow and slid her chair out so she was facing me.

"Yeah sure, what's up?"

"Well we uh, didn't use a condom. I've always used one before so I don't have anything I can pass onto you, I was just wondering if you were-"

"I'm on the pill, don't worry. I've been it when I starting thinking up of my experiment and I don't have anything to pass onto you either. " She smiled, "Um, well since were on the topic... I was wondering if you would want to go out for a drink or dinner or something while we discuss my experiment?"

"Yes, that'd be a good idea. How about tonight? We can finish up early and head out for dinner at seven o'clock? How does that sound?" I asked.

"That sounds great, I definitely need to go home to change out of these clothes, not to mention that I'm going commando right now." She laughed.

Oh shit, I completely forgot I had her thong in my pocket. Mmm, maybe this could be to my advantage. I smirked at her and started walking up to her, she had the most adorable confused face.

"What're you doing Jake?"

"You shouldn't have reminded me you weren't wearing panties."

"Jake someone could come in!"

"That didn't stop you before baby." I replied trailing my nose up the side of her neck smelling her faint perfume. I knew for a fact that no one would come in, I'd specifically told everyone that we weren't to be disturbed unless it was urgent and even then they should just call Sasha's office. Although the thrill was still there.

I walked behind Sasha's chair and moved my mouth to her ear. "Don't move." I whispered and I heard her moan and close her eyes. I slid my hands down her neck to her shoulders circling them, massaging her stiff shoulders. She leaned back tilting her head against my stomach and giving me a gorgeous view down her blouse.

I licked my lips and slipped my hands into her blouse and into her bra cups using my fingers on both hands to roll her nipples between them. Her chest was rising and falling and I was getting harder at her surrender to me. How can she affect me without even doing anything!?

"Mmm, Jake. Fuck that feels soooo goood." She moaned groaning the end of her sentence. I smirked and leaned forward taking her earlobe between my teeth and biting it gently while continuing to pinch her nipples.

All of a sudden I pull my hands out and spin her chair around so she's facing me. I kneel down and lift her skirt up to her waist and slowly spread her legs apart. I could smell her arousal and see that she was wet. Fuck me, she should just never wear panties ever again!

I wanted to go slow and give her a little torture, I know I went fast earlier so now I was going to take my time. I slowly glided my hands up her smooth thighs and spread her as far as the chair would allow and used my thumb to slowly rub her clit. I hear her gasp and I swear she has the sexiest voice, even if it's groaning or moaning.

Licking my way up her thighs I follow the trail from my hands and used the tip of my tongue to flick her clit. By now she was on edge and was soaking wet for me, for me to drink her juices, and I obliged. I circled her pussy with my tongue while massaging her clit with my fingers and all the while she's filling my ears wither lustful moans.

I switched to licking her clit and pressed two fingers into her channel only slightly. Sucking and drinking her juices and I stop my teasing and plunge my fingers deep inside her channel. Her hips jerk forward and I use my other arm to lay it across her hips and hold her down.

I start thrusting my fingers faster and faster and circling them feeling her walls hitting her bundle of nerves over and over again. Her walls begin tightening around my fingers, clamping down and pulling them deeper.

Just then the phone rings and she groans in frustration. "Jake... Oh God! Jake stop, the phone Ah!"

I smile and take my mouth off her and slow down my thrusts but don't stop. "Answer it, Sasha."

She looks down at me with wide eyes and shakes her head. "Answer it!" I demand, thrusting in harder and fast.

"Oh God!" She moans and lifts the receiver. "Jake.. Uh, Jacob Stone's ooooffice! Saahhhhhsha speaking, how may I help you?" She tried to sound professional, but I want to her fall apart. I remove my finger and instead thrust my tongue up inside of her and lick up her whole pussy gulping her wetness before plunging my fingers back inside of her.

She covers the receiver and moans like crazy before trying to hit my hand away. I laugh and just continue my torture.

"Uh huh, uh huh... uh OHHHHH huh. No, no I'm fine. Ok, Well Mr Stone is... uh busy right now. I'll get HIM to call you back. Ok BYE!" She says to the person on the phone before slamming the receiver down so hard it falls off the desk.

She grabs my hair and tugs hard but not enough to hurt. I'm so proud of her for even finishing the call so I reward her with stroking her her g-spot over and over while snaking my other hand up to massage her breast.

Sasha start grinding against my hands, her juices soaking my knuckles and I feel her orgasm building up. Her walls tighten again and I feel her whole core shake and her body stiffen. She screams out my name into her hand that's clamped over her mouth and then slump down into her chair.

"Holy... holy... fuck me, that was just... oh my God!" She pants with her eyes closed.

"Mmm, that was definitely worth missing out on paperwork for" I tell her, just marvelling at how addictive her moaning is.

She laughed. "Oh definitely! You better watch out, I might become addicted to getting orgasms from you." She joked.

"Well, you ask anytime. I'm more than happy to give it to you." I replied with a wink.

She opens her eyes and zeros down at my major boner.

"Or maybe I can be the one to give it to you." Her sultry voice offers. She stands up and grips my shoulders pushing me down into her chair. She walked over to lock the door, I mean hey we were lucky before we might as well not push our luck. And sways her hips over to me.

"Ever had sex in a chair before stud?" She asks toying with the hem of her skirt, bringing it high enough for me to glimpse her bare pussy.

"No actually…" I trail off, hypnotized by the sight of her hands. She slips her hand under her skirt and holds it up with the hand. She uses a finger to draw a path across her mound and her circles her clit.

"You have no idea how good you are at eating pussy Jake. It makes me want to explode." She explains while slowly, oh so slowly, dips her finger into her channel. Oh my God! That is so fucking hot! She then pumps it and circles it around a little before taking out popping it into her mouth and moans.

I'm so close to exploding just by watching her little display that I shift myself to ease some of the pressure. Sasha walks over to the chair and unzips my fly pulling my pants and my boxers down. She then bends down and licks my erection from the base to the tip swirling it around and hitting that sensitive ridge connecting the head to my shaft and I moan out loud.

"Sasha, you better hurry up and not tease me, I'm so close I don't know how I'm not coming right now!" I growl through clenched teeth. She smiles a tantalizing smile and straddles me on the chair.

"Well then, I guess I'll just have to fuck your brains out then Mr Stone." She whispered huskily in my ear before quickly sliding my erection into her tight, hot pussy. She begins to bounce up and down, stroking my shaft and bringing me closer to my orgasm.

Finally I couldn't take it and I grab her with her behind the knees with my forearms and stand up. She squeals and quickly throws her hands backwards holding onto the edge of her desk so that she basically lying in midair.

I throw her legs over my shoulders and begin slamming into her hard and fast and all too quickly I feel the tightening in my stomach and the warmth rush out of me. Her walls clamp down on me as she comes at the same time I roll my hips around making her orgasm last longer and heighten the pleasure for both of us.

After a minute I pull her up so I'm carrying her, still inside of her and kiss her hungrily. She kisses back with as much hunger and enthusiasm. Afterwards I pull out slowly and slide her down my body loving the feeling then tuck her hair behind her ear.

"I say we finish up now before I take you again Miss Montgomery."

Sasha's POV

Fu-cking –Hell.

I think I may have died and gone to orgasm heaven!

"I think we should finish now before I take you again Miss Montgomery." I hear Jake say.

I nod my head not trusting my voice just yet and give him one last kiss. Boy can that man rock my world.

We finish off whatever was urgent to do today and switch off our computers. He waits for me by the door while I grab my bag and blazer and we descend down to the car park in silence. I check my watch and see that it reads three o'clock. Wow we really did leave early!

"So I'll just pick you up at your place at quarter to seven. I made a booking for Fraîche at seven." He says.

"Oh wow, I hear that place is really yummy and hard to get a seat in. How did you manage to get us a table on such short notice?" I ask. He shrugs his shoulders and just smiles at me indicating that it was his little secret. I rolled my eyes and smile back. "Ok, well I'll see you in a few hours Jake."

He waves goodbye and we walk off to our cars.

When I arrive home, I walk in my apartment loving the homely feeling it has and fall onto the sofa. I can't believe I'm actually doing this, I can't believe I'm sleeping around with the notorious Jacob Stone. I smile to myself and check the time. I have just under three hours to get ready, nice.

Deciding that I need to relax my already too relaxed muscles I run a bath and add lots of bubbles. I soak in the tub for about an hour reading my current romance book, yeah I read a lot of romance books, adding a little more hot water everytime it gets too cold.

When I finish I wrap myself up in a big fluffy white towel and dry off the soothing water and leftover bubbles that clung to my damp skin. Hmm, what to wear? I didn't want to look like I was trying too hard or look too casual. Fraîche was a high class restaurant that, without Jake, I wouldn't even have been able to get into. I decide to go with a deep blue dress that flared out to above my knees. It had a sweetheart neckline and a low back that dipped halfway down. I clipped the black belt that sat around my waistline making my figure look delicious then I stared at the mirror. Not too shabby, if I say so myself.

I dusted on grey eye shadow and swiped some mascara on framing my eyes. I added a little blush before slicking on a nude lipstick. I left my hair down tonight seeing as I never usually do and just swept it over my shoulder before adding a long silver necklace and diamond studs. By the time I finished getting ready it was 7:40 and I was contemplating on two different pumps to wear. The intercom buzzed and I ran over to check who it was, though it was easily Jake.

"Hello?"

"Hey Sweet cheeks, it's Jake."

"You might as well stay down there, I'll just grab my shoes and meet you outside."

"Ok sure."

I decided just to go with my 5 inch black stilettos, I mean, we'll be sitting down for the most of it anyways, grabbed my purse and locked up walking to the elevators. I was nervous. I couldn't believe he agreed to my guinea pig for this experiment. Though if today had anything to go by how we suited in bed then we have no problem. I sighed, but when I'm around him I totally lose myself. I'm supposed to be taking notes and pleasuring HIM, not the other way around.

I reached the lobby and the doors opened. I saw him immediately through the glass doors leaning against his car. He looked so edible it was insane. He wore a black suit with a black undershirt and looked like a panther lounging in all his glory. Do not drool Sasha!

I walked forward feigning confidence and noticed that he was staring at my body and had yet to reach my face. God it's going to be so hard to resist him, how the hell did I manage to resist him for entire time I've known him?!

Jake's POV

I was leaning against the hood of my car waiting for Sasha to come down. I couldn't stop reminiscing about how hot she was at the office. She literally turned into a completely different woman and the thought that she was both uptight, efficient secretary and sexy, wanton sex Goddess was mind blowing.

Just then I see the elevator doors open and a high heeled clad leg steps out. My mouth waters at how long these legs were, they seemed to reach forever! Shit, I realise that it's actually Sasha and fuck me she looks too tempting in her outfit. There was enough cleavage to tease me with and taper down to a tiny waist and then splays out to womanly hips. Then back to those legs, oh God those legs!

I tear my eyes away from her decadent body and see that she's checking me out as well. Well at least it's not just me! I feel a stirring in my pants, that can't be good. She's going to kill me I swear! She walks through the doors and gives me a shy little wave.

"Hey Jake" she greets me.

"Good evening beautiful." I reply making her blush. Mmm, I wonder how far I can make her blush? Came an evil thought, I smile and tucked the thought away for later. "You look absolutely amazing Sasha"

She smiled and did a little twirl showing me her backless dress. My jaw nearly dropped. Nearly! I managed to get a hold of myself and hold on to a little dignity while down below my stirring became a full erection.

"You like it?" She asks me with a cheeky smile.

"It's making me a different kind of hungry if that's what you mean." I say huskily.

I open the door of the car for her and shut her door before walking over to the driver side. The drive to the restaurant was pleasant and we spoke about work and family. When we reached the restaurant I paid for valet and walked her in guiding her with my hand on her lower back using my thumb to stroke the bare pare of her back.

Once we were seated and ordered drinks and our food we relaxed. I'd asked for a table that was secluded and they obliged placing us in the corner that was hidden by plants and lights. We were seated next to a glass panel that over looked the water and the view was quite dazzling.

I turned my attention back to the beauty sitting in front of me and just took in her features. The soft glow of the lights gave her a soft look. She was gazing at the water with her chin propped up on her clasped hands.

"You really do look beautiful Sasha." I say, breaking her attention from the view.

"Thank you Jake, but... that's really not necessary." She says dropping her gaze to the table cloth as if it held something interesting.

"What do you mean 'not necessary'" I ask curiously.

"The compliments. I mean this experiment is about how I can pleasure a man and how to keep his eyes from wondering away from me especially whenever I do get pregnant."

I was shocked. She didn't believe me? I guess what with all those bastards cheating on her and ruining her confidence in herself she would have a low self esteem. She always seemed so confident in the office that I never realised how broken she felt. I reached out and grasped her hands between mine. From the outside it would look as though we were lovers sharing an intimate moment.

"I'm beings serious Sasha. I've always thought of you as a beautiful and confident woman. Just the way you hold yourself at the office, you don't even realise the beauty you have. And the way you dress tonight completely blows my mind. I mean look at you. You look completely different and that's just another type of beautiful. " I told her.

I started rubbing my thumb around her hand in a circular motion, "You're not wearing glasses tonight?" I asked.

She ducked her head and blushed, I love that blush, really I do.

"Oh, yeah. I just thought I'd try contacts. They're not too bad but it took me about five minutes getting them in. Do I look weird?" She gushed scrunching her face.

"In no way could you ever look weird. It just... You have beautiful eyes, the deepest emerald green I've ever seen." I replied staring deep into her eyes.

She stared back before snapping herself out of her reverie and cleared her throat. "I uh, I guess we should start on the experiment." I replied with a nod and leaned back against my chair. "So basically I did some research on what men find pleasurable before and during sex. You know things like foreplay, toys, fantasies, role playing and positions.

So what I've done is compile a few things into a survey for you to answer so I can get the gist before... um, putting it into practice." Her face became the colour of ripe strawberries and she fidgeted as though to fix the non-existent glasses.

She then proceeded to take out a piece of paper and a pen. "So uh, I'm just going to ask you a few questions and all you have to do is answer truthfully." We were interrupted by our food being placed down and we both thanked the waiter.

I took a sip of my drink and waved my hand. "How about we discuss this over dessert, if you like. For now I'd like to enjoy your company."

"Oh I'm sorry, yes that sounds like a great idea."

We ate our meals, making comfortable conversation . I was entranced by the way her mouth. The way her lips curled around her spoon and plumped together and give an unconscious mewing sound when she enjoyed the taste of her food. Even the way she licked her lips whenever she sipped her wine and I constantly had to fight with my inner self to stop thinking of those lips doing that to a particular part of my anatomy.

For dessert she ordered a raspberry cheesecake and I ordered the decadent chocolate cake. After the waiter left we got back to topic.

"Ok, say I believe you have some questions for me." I offered.

"Right, right. Yes um... ok" She bends down again to grab the paper and pen. "What's your favourite position during sex?"

"Any."

"Could you be more specific? Is it missionary, from behind, standing up, girl on top anything else?"

"I like them all. All positions feel good and I don't really like one more than the other."

She scribbled something on the paper, "Ok, not really helpful all right" She laughed, "Do you have any fantasies? There are several listed down such as threesomes, anal, sex games stuff like that."

"How about I make it easy for you, Sasha? What I find pleasurable in bed is having just me and the woman in question. No toys, no other person, just me and her touching and kissing and knowing I, alone, was able to bring her climax."

Sasha's POV

Oh wow. Jake was painting a sexual picture in my head that I was having a hard time getting out. I was breathing heavily, my chest rising and falling, his eyes were boring into mine making his announcement clear.

"Ok," I squeaked. "Um, how about role playing? Any particular roles you find or would find interesting? I've read somewhere that a particularly popular one is sex with a mermaid."

"A mermaid?" He asked a bit amused.

"Yes, you know being lost sea with no female companion then out of nowhere a beautiful half naked woman appears and offers you sex. But the tricky part is that she's half fish so I guess most of it would be foreplay and oral?" We both laughed, when I read that I found it interestingly bizarre.

"Well, as interesting as that sounds I'm more of a realistic lover. So no role playing, really."

I laughed, "You know Jake, you're not really very helpful with my survey. How about you just tell me what you like then?"

"Hmm ok, I find it highly erotic when a woman experiments during sex, when she finds out what I like and pleasures me over and over that way. I love it when a woman wears her hair down so that I can tangle my hands in it and guide her mouth to where I want it. Dirty talk never goes a miss though it's not everyone cup of tea. Hmm..." I was mentally writing the list down and imagining myself surrendering to his wishes while he leaned back and thought about what gets him hot and bothered. "I guess I find what I like depending on the woman I'm with."

"Yeah.., very true."

He leaned forward, placing his elbows on the table and looked straight into my soul. "So Miss Montgomery, what turns you on?"

3

CHAPTER 3

Sasha's POV

"So Miss Montgomery, what turns you on?" Jake asked me huskily as he stared deep into my eyes.

The question caught me by surprise and he smirked while I collected my thoughts.

"Me? You want know what turns me on?" I asked, astounded that the great Jacob Stone would want to know my little pleasurable secrets."Uh... I, I don't really know?" I answered.

"I guess that means we'll have to be doing a lot of exploring together then"

"No, Jake. I don't think you understand what my experiment is about. It's about me being able to pleasure a man so that I can be good enough that he doesn't cheat on me. I've had enough of that shit and I'm not about to continue my life with one cheating asshole after the next. It doesn't matter that I don't know exactly know what I find pleasurable in bed to list down and it certainly isn't about you having to pleasure me. It's about me pleasuring you." I told him firmly.

He chuckled, and I lifted an eyebrow in response. "Sasha, I think you're the one who's wrong here. Men find it pleasurable when they can pleasure the woman too, it lifts their egos and in return, turns them on. It also does matter if you know what pleasures you because we, as men, can use that to our advantage."

Hmm, I never thought of it that way. I churned his words around my head pondering about I found really pleasuring for myself. I was interrupted by Jake trailing his finger down the side of my cheek. I closed my eyes and tilted my neck as he continued trailing it down the side of my neck and across my collarbone. He swept it across my cleavage and then it was gone.

I snapped my eyes open and saw him gazing at me, pupils dark and dilated.

"Stop thinking so hard Sasha. This is pleasure we're talking about, it comes naturally and I'll even be the one to help you" he winked, though I knew he meant it on a deeper level.

Jake insisted on paying the bill then dropped me home.

"We should do this more often" he told me as he held his hand out while helping me from the car. I smiled and agreed. I would love to spend more time out of the office with him, though I suppose now I'll be getting a LOT of extra after hour time with him.

"So uh... would you like to come up for some coffee or something?" I asked him trying to be coy.

"Or something... but coffee will suffice" he replied cheekily. He drove off to park the car and I waited for him before the both of us entered the elevator. As we waited in the elevator I held in my urges to just pounce on him and take him right then right there. His scent swirled around me in the confined space and the warmth from his body radiated from him. The door opened and I quickly strode to my apartment letting us in.

"So how do you like your coffee?" I called out to Jake from the kitchen taking down two mugs from the cupboard. Suddenly two muscled arms appeared on either side of me and latched their hands on the edge on the counter. Jake trailed his nose down my neck breathing in deeply.

"Have I ever told you how decadent you smell?" I whispered into my ear.

"No..." I gasped.

He switched to peppering slow tortuous kisses up and down my neck, sucking with each kiss then swept my hair to the side and kept his kissing torture as he kissed the back of my neck sending shivers down my spine. Following the shivers he kissed, sucked and lightly bit a path down my exposed back.

The sensations he was forcing on me were enthralling. My eye lids fell and I arched my back with every nip of his teeth on my sensitive skin. I was still trapped between his arms and even though he was slowly torturing me with his mouth no other part of his body touched me.

I felt the tip of his hot tongue slide its way back up my spine and he brought his lips next to my ear.

"I think, instead of finding out how I like my coffee, we should find out what you find pleasurable" he whispered, his breath blowing the tendrils back and forth. I moaned. I couldn't help it; I was in no shape to talk. He was inflicting so many sensations and I just needed more of him.

Jake's POV

Her womanly scent filled my nostrils arousing me even more. I'd been on edge all night and when she invited me up for coffee I jumped at the chance. Now with her between my arms I wanted to do everything and anything all night and possibly all tomorrow as well.

I pushed my chest against her and my erection prodded the bottom of her ass. I was just itching to plunge into and fuck her like tomorrow, especially with all the talk about sex and foreplay during dessert. I slid my hands up her smooth arms and I felt her lean against me making me smile. I continued my journey up to her shoulders and massaged her, rubbing all her tension away from her.

She'd told me that she didn't know what she found pleasurable and I was making it my mission to find out. She wanted to pleasure her future man in bed and in order to really connect sexually she'd need to know what she liked. The thought of her with another man made me clench my teeth but I otherwise tried to ignore the shots of jealousy shooting through my veins.

After all her knots were gone I slid my hands over her full breasts and kneaded them through her dress. Damn this dress! Her nipples poked through her material and I smirked at her reaction to my hands. I could hear her breathing deepening and little mews of content escaping her delectable little mouth. I then continued moving my hands down south caressing her soft, taut skin of her stomach then brushing over her thighs squeezing her toned legs and grinding into her from behind.

"God Jake please!" Sasha moaned as she pushed her ass against my throbbing dick. She was driving me insane but I wanted to touch her everywhere, kiss her everywhere and lick her everywhere so she knew what she wanted.

I slowly push the dress from her shoulders, kissing every newly exposed skin. I kept everything slow and tortuous, I wanted her to scream my name in frustration and demand that I give her what she needed. Her dress was now down to her waist and I swallowed loudly as I pushed the blue material over her hips and watched it pool around her pretty feet. She stood in front of me in her midnight blue thong and no bra and I swear I could've come right then and there.

"Do you like this baby?" I whispered as I circled her clit with my fingers spreading her juices around her dripping pussy.

"Oh yes Jake, yes! Please don't make me wait!" she groaned.

I smiled and shook my head nuzzling the side of her neck. "Sorry baby, but this all for you."

The tips of my fingers played at her entrance, poking in then escaping out, her juices dripping with desire and filling the room with her arousal. Without warning I plunged my fingers in deep and she arched her back leaning in to me panting with every thrust of my fingers. I was so hard that I was thrusting my dick at the same time I was thrusting my fingers into her tightening channel. Her walls her squeezing my fingers and I could tell she was close, I bit her neck where it connected to her shoulders and she cried out in ecstasy before slumping forward and catching herself on the kitchen counter.

"Holy shit Jake that was amazing!" she panted.

"We're nowhere near finished baby"

I turned her around to face me and lifted her up, her legs circled my waist and I could feel my erection prodding against her thong clad pussy still wet from her climax. I carried her down the hall looking for her room and slid her down my body.

"Why am I the only one naked?" she said huskily with a coy smirk.

"You're not naked" I answered back nodding towards her thong. My eyes widened when she walked backwards to the edge of her bed and slowly slid her thong down her long legs then opened her legs wide letting me see the glistening lips of her pussy.

"I love it when you touch me Jake, it makes me so fucking wet for you, even just a look and I feel like creaming right there and then" As she spoke she played with her pussy, massaging her swollen clit and arching her back. It was by far the most erotic thing I've seen and damn did it make me even harder and want to fuck her brain out!

"Yeah? What else do you like baby?" I choked out subconsciously rubbing the front of my straining pants.

"Well I like it when I'm not the only one naked for one..." she replied staring straight into my eyes, "Strip Jake, I want you naked. Now."

Oh hell yeah, I love dirty talk and I have a feeling she loves it too. I stripped off my shirt and pants along with my boxers and stood naked in front of her, my swollen dick begging for attention. She purred and licked her licked her lips eyeing my erection and held a finger up motioning for me to go to her. I complied.

"Jake, you know this is not about me, it's supposed to be all about you. So tell me... what do you want me to do to you?" She whispered huskily.

I laid on the bed on my back and watched her crawl up my body swishing those sexy hips and biting her swollen lip. "I think you know what I want baby"

She smiled and planted her hands on either side of my hips before dipping her head down and licked from the bottom of my balls to the tip of my erection in one slow lick. She started pumping my dick with two hands and teasing the hell out of me by concentrating her sucks on the head of my erection and I just couldn't take it!

"Bring your ass up here Sasha! I want to taste you while you eat my cock"

I pulled her hips up so she was laying on top of me with her never letting go my erection and as she started deep throating me I plunged my tongue into her channel while massaging her clit and lapping at her lips. I moaned at the taste of her warm juices and she grinded her pussy into my face as she moaned back sending vibrations from her mouth through my cock and making my body go crazy!

I thrusted into her mouth and she grinded against my face harder as I slipped two fingers in and began pumping her pussy to get her to reach her climax. Suddenly she orgasmed and deep throated me at the same time and I panted through it so I wouldn't burst. When she finished I slid out from under her and held her hips so I was behind her and she was on her knees.

I leaned over and grabbed her swinging breasts while sliding my throbbing cock over her juices and rubbing her clit.

"I'm going to fuck you so hard you're going to scream my name in pleasure and beg for me to do it again" then before she had the time to gasp I plunged my swollen dick into her and began thrusting at high speed holding onto her hips her dear life. She was panting and groaning and screaming for me not to stop.

I felt her pussy tighten and I was done for! We climaxed at the same time screaming each other's name and I pushed deeper as I sprayed my seed into her and we collapsed together on the bed. I stayed there for a few seconds before rolling us to our sides so I wouldn't crush her.

"Holy. Shit! Ho-ly. Shit!" she panted over and over making me smile.

"You can say that again!" I laughed.

We stayed in that position just catching our breaths before she turned around to face me. She lifted her leg and rested it on top of my hip before cuddling up to me. I didn't think she meant for it to be sexual, just to make herself more comfortable, but that didn't mean I didn't react to her goddess body.

My dick was hardening at just the thought of being so close to her pussy again. I groaned, she really was going to kill me! We haven't even technically started her experiment yet!

My erection nudged her thigh and she looked up at me in surprise making me laugh.

"Sorry, I can't help it. You're just too damn sexy for your own good, just ignore it." I told her.

She didn't.

Instead she straddled me and slipped my erection straight into her womanhood. There was no playing around this time. She was playing with her breasts and pinching her nipples as she bounced up and down on me. My hands immediately went to her hips and helped her up and down.

It was a fast coupling and she was soon crying in pleasure as her climax took her to new heights, I grinded her to me and circled her hips to prolong it and she was soon panting in another orgasm. I flipped her over and placed bother legs over my shoulders as I pounded into her over and over. I bent down to kiss her mouth and she opened her mouth to me letting me slip my tongue in. She sucked my tongue and I exploded into her.

She fell asleep with me spooning her from behind and I couldn't help a sigh. What was she doing to me? I breathed in her sweet smell and wondered if I'd be able to let her go when her little experiment was finished.

4

CHAPTER 4

Sasha's POV

It was the beginning of a new week. Hell week to be exact.

I rolled over to my side and watched the morning sunlight lazily grow brighter every minute through the blinds. I sighed, for once in my life I didn't feel like working. I'd had the most magical weekend and I could definitely feel it in my muscles.

Jake slept over after our uh... coffee, and I was ecstatic that nothing was awkward. He was a beautiful sight to see first thing in the morning and definitely better to feel as well. We had sex twice more before our breakfast then he finally pried himself away from me to head back home. I sighed. My bed felt much too cold and big without him.

My thoughts headed back to work again. Damnit. Hell week was our busiest week of the year and no doubt with business booming that this week would be our busiest yet. There would be meetings to attend, papers to file and write out and ergh, I didn't even want to think of it.

I rolled myself out of bed and stretched my stiff muscles and headed to the shower.

I walked out of the elevator, wearing white slacks and a black silk sleeveless with a slight ruffle around the neckline and my white blazer. It was unusually cold for this time of year and was forecasted to stay that way. It was like the seasons were merging into one and were saying 'to hell with normal seasonal weather, let's fuck shit up'!

I bought Starbucks for myself and Jake so I left his on his desk and started on with my day.

"Urgh! Talk about living through hell!" I complained to Jake as we finally finished Hell Week

"Tell me about it" he grumbled rubbing a rough hand over his tired face, "I need a vacation. Or at least get the hell away from this office. "

I agreed but felt a little disheartened. We'd become so close ever since he agreed to my experiment. I haven't even been able to start it!

"I know, how about you and I go to my private island next week? A whole week of nothing but sunshine and bikinis" he winked at me eyeing my body. I shivered at the darkening of his eyes.

"I don't know" I pretended to think about it, "I'm not sure you'd suit a bikini all that well, despite how amazing your body is" he laughed and shook his head. "I'd love to go with you, so long as my boss says it's all right to go"

"Hmm, I'm sure your boss will let it slide this time. You've been working very hard, it's time you relax and be a little naughty" he replied winking at me.

I was too excited!

T only times I'd been overseas were for business and now here I was on my way to the airport to board Jake's private jet.

I'd dressed in a simple short white summer dress that showed my cleavage nicely and white sandals. Since it was still a bit chilly I had a yellow wrap around me shoulders. The cab stopped outside the airport and helped me with my baggage; I tipped him and rolled my luggage inside to meet with Jake.

"You know, you should've accepted the car I wanted to send you so you didn't need a cab." I heard a deep masculine voice whisper in my ear.

"I'm no spoilt brat like some hunky billionaires." I joked.

He laughed and took the luggage from me. We were able to bypass everyone and all lines and headed straight for his private jet. In no time we were pulling out and starting to ascend.

"Mmm, I love the feeling when the plane takes off. Landing, however, is a totally different situation." I said closing my eyes and revelling in the tingly feeling in my stomach from the take off. Jake didn't say anything so I peeked through my eyes and sneaked a look at him. It wasn't missed because he was staring openly at me not saying a word.

"Is everything ok, Jake?" I asked.

"You're so beautiful, Sasha. I still get shocked whenever I see you out of your business outfits. I love this chilled and relaxed Sasha. It definitely suits your personality." I blushed at his sudden compliments and smiled.

"Thank you Jake, that's incredibly sweet of you."

For the next half hour we spoke about anything besides work, we wanted nothing to do with work so we avoided the subject like the plague. An idea hit me.

"So Jake, I was thinking since we'll be relaxing from work for the next week that it'd be the perfect time to kick-start my experiment." I smiled coyly and I could see the cogs in his working in his head about what I meant.

"I think that's an excellent idea" he agreed a smirk sliding onto his face.

"Good." Then without a word I stood up and straddled him on his seat.

"Holy shit, I didn't you meant now." He cried startled.

"One of the most popular fantasies is having sex in a plane midair, you know, to be a part of the mile high club." I mumbled while bending forward and gently biting his earlobe. My ears were greeted with a low moan and I felt him shift lower in his seat so that his growing bulge was nudging my thigh.

"Have you ever had sex in a plane before Jake?" I whispered as I peppered kisses down his neck and licked his Adams apple. I felt it bobble up and down as he swallowed.

"Uh, no..." was the response I got out of him. I smiled against his skin.

"Well then, I guess I'll have to introduce you to the mile high club."

Smashed my lips against his and his mouth opened allowing my tongue to caress his tongue in a passionate dance. His moan vibrated down my throat and reached my core making it tighten in excitement.

I began rubbing my core against his now hard bulge and damn did I miss it! I grabbed his hand and tangled it in my hair, which I left down after remembering that he loved it, and whispered huskily in his ear.

"Show me what you want."

Jake's POV

Oh shit! This woman is making my fantasy come true. I never really thought of myself as having a fantasy but with her on my lap and telling me to do exactly what I loved doing was seriously sexy.

I tightened my grip on her hair and pulled it roughly back but not enough to hurt her. Her slender neck was opened to me so I bent forward to lick from her collarbone up to her jaw. I opened my legs wider and she slipped down to her knees dragging her breasts down my chests and rubbed it against my groin. Fuck me!

She unzipped my jeans and kissed my erection through my boxers. It twitched at her touch and I needed more. She pulled my boxers down and began playing with my dick. She toyed with it, experimenting with stroking with one and two hands then switching to stroking and caressing my balls.

"Sasha!" I warned her, she knew what she was doing to me. I was harder than a steel pole and she hadn't taken me into her mouth yet.

"Show me" was all she said staring deep into my eyes. I guided her mouth to the tip of my throbbing erection and a pearl moisture appeared.

"Lick it baby" I instructed her.

She obliged and swirled her tongue over the glistening tip and. Her mouth was hot and wet and I was dying for more!

"Now stroke my dick with your tongue and savour it" I'd never instructed a woman before and even though Sasha was unbelievable at giving head, instructing her felt erotic and was so hot.

She slowly brought the head into her mouth and sucked slightly, with my hand in her hair I pumped her mouth to a steady rhythm and I couldn't even explain how amazing it felt. I was throbbing inside her mouth and her moaning was sending vibrations throughout my body and I was so close to blowing.

"Do you like it baby?" I gasped. She mumbled an 'uh huh' and she began taking control. She pumped her mouth and stroked her hands over my entire erection.

"Oh shit! Baby, I'm going to come." I warned her and tried to pry her mouth away. She wouldn't have any of that and opened her eyes staring straight into mine holding them as she sucked me. The connection between us was intensified and I threw my head back and orgasmed.

She sucked it all in and a few moments later she was kissing her way up my body to peck my lips.

"Holy shit baby girl!" I gasped, my chest heaving up and down, "That was... amazing!!"

She winked and circled her finger around the head of my dick again and I moaned.

"You know, that doesn't really count as the mile high club." I joked.

"Oh we're not done yet..." She stood up and continued with slowly slipping her straps off and letting the dress fall down her sexy body. She was standing there in her strapless white bra and white lace thong and a twirl. "You like?"

I nodded with my mouth open and I must've looked like an idiot because she giggled and closed my mouth with a finger. Her eyes dared me to follow her as she walked towards the room at the back of the plane and she unclasped her bra letting it fall and leave her tong clad ass and bare back on display.

She entered the room and closed the door slightly letting me hear the springs of the queen bed bear her weight. What the fuck? What the hell am I still doing here?! I stood and nearly fell as I rushed to the room with my jeans and boxers still leaving my growing manhood for show.

The view that welcomed me was a man's wet dream.

She was lying on her back on the bed her full breasts on display as she pinched her nipples and rubbed the lace that covered her pussy. Holy hell!! I shook myself out my trance and scolded myself for acting like a teenager who'd never seen a naked woman before.

I strolled forward until I reached the bed and circled my hands around her ankles before stroking it up her legs.

"Well Captain, I think it's about time I give you your wings for the mile high club" she said huskily.

I smiled and shook my head, "Not yet."

I trailed my hands up her calves, behind her knees and rubbed her quivering thighs. I could smell her scent and it was driving me mad. It was like all my primal urges were rising and I needed to take her, to brand her. To make her mine.

I slid two fingers in her wet core and she arched her back moaning. I pumped my fingers and crawled up to her kissing her lips inhaling all the hormones she was releasing. She lost it and next thing I knew she was tearing at my t-shirt, pulling it above my head and using her feet to kick my jeans and boxers down. That was so God damn sexy!

"Fuck me, Jake! Fuck me nice and hard. Make me explode, I want you so bad!" She cried and it was my undoing. I wanted to bury my face in her pussy and taste her til she exploded but we both couldn't wait!

I rubbed the head of my cock around her soaking pussy and tore her lace thong off, woops I guess she can't use them anymore. Her heat was seeping into me and I pushed into her so slowly she was whimpering. She grabbed my ass and pulled me to her tightly I lost my breath momentarily. Dam, I don't think I could ever get over how amazing she felt around me.

"You're tight Sasha, God you feel a so good" Then I was gone. I thrust into her over and over stroking my erection against her inner walls and relishing her moans and cries of pleasure. Her walls tightened around my cock and milked me for all I had. We climaxed at the same time and I collapsed on top of her gasping for breath. It was a few minutes before either of us spoke.

"Welcome to the mile high club Jake" She smiled. I laughed and kissed her lips.

"Glad to be here."

The plane shook and the wind outside hit the plane. All of a sudden the plane tilted and we rolled off the bed, I rolled so I could take most of the impact and held her close. We waited for the shaking to pass I helped her up.

"Sorry about that Sir and Mam, there was a bit of turbulence but that should be all of it for now. It might be best to fasten your seat belts, arrival will be in twenty minutes." The pilot's voice announced over the speakers

We burst out laughing and began getting dressed. My mind wondered to her body when I remembered that she won't be wearing underneath her dress. Don't even go there Jake.

We got seated and she threw a coy smile and a wink before buckling herself in.

In no time at all the plane was descending and I looked outside the window at the beautiful view below us. The tropical island was surrounded by sparkling clear blue water, fading from clear to dark blue. Dolphins and whales and other such marine animals were visible and I couldn't wait to see them up close.

As the wheels touched ground and the doors opened up I took a deep breath in and inhaled the warm air that smelled vaguely of palm trees and sea salt. Jake took hold of my elbow and we made our way to his summer house.

I smiled. Let the experiment officially begin.

5

— ◆ —

CHAPTER 5

Jake's summer house was a sight to see. It wasn't the obnoxious house I imagined it to be, but instead it was sort of a cottage that blended in so perfectly with the island. The porch encircled around the entire one storey house and had little fans that looked like woven handmade fans together.

There were bamboo woven furniture with puffy cushions which would be perfect for lazing about on a hot day like today. Palm trees sprouted out all around the area and swayed back and forth in a slow dance. I absolutely loved it and I haven't even seen the inside.

Jake opened the door then stepped back letting me walk through first, such a gentleman, and I gasped. It was so cute inside and so much bigger than what the outside showed.

"Would you like a tour?" I heard Jake ask putting our luggage down by the door.

"Oh, please!" I almost clapped with excitement and flashed him a huge grin.

"Right this way then m'lady" Jake showed me all the different rooms and even offered a history of the island and the cottage.

I was so entranced by his knowledge of everything here and wondered if this was the life he'd rather live than the busy city life we both live day to day in.

We walked down a narrow hallway that was lined with dusty photo frames filled with family photos, one of them even had a picture of me. I traced my finger over my young face leaving a streak of dust where I rubbed.

"When was this?" I asked Jake. It was a picture of me and Jenna laughing and making faces at the camera while our faces and clothes were completely splattered with food.

"That was after you and Jenna graduated from high school remember? We had a barbeque at our place and, I don't even remember how, but a food fight started and you two wreaked havoc over everyone else." He told me chuckling at the memory.

"Oh that right!" I laughed, how could forget such a day!

Jake continued to show me what was down the hall and then he pushed open a door. The room was painted a sky blue and the thick carpet was a dark blue, almost as though they wanted to capture the scenery outside. The huge king size four poster bed was situated in the centre with pure white sheets and white mosquito netting pulled back.

The dresser and side tables were made of wood and there even an ensuite and the closet was tucked in the corner of the room.

"This is your room, if you choose to use it" he winked, "and my room is next door. I'll bring your luggage in and let you freshen up before I show you the last part. It's my favourite part of the house. There's fresh towels in the bathroom, make yourself at home." He offered one more smile and closed the door after pulling my luggage in.

Wow, this place was so amazing, I could just live here forever!

I showered letting the cool water chase away the sweat and dirt on my body before slipping into one of my new bikinis. I'd gone on a shopping spree and bought skimpy bikinis and clothes that would turn his head as well as a multitude of lingerie.

This particular bikini was not as bad as the others. I still felt a little self conscious and I wanted to build up to this experiment slowly, for my sake. It was black with silver hoops between my breasts and sides of my hips but the bottoms were small and showed my ass quite nicely.

I slipped on a loose white singlet and yellow short shorts then stepped into my flip flops before tying my hair into a messy bun. It was a bit too hot to leave it down. With nothing else to do I walked outside.

"Jake?" I called out, but there was no answer. I heard the faint spray of his shower from his room and grinned. Oh yeah.

I opened the door to his room and slipped inside closing it quietly. His room was much like mine only his walls were a darker blue than mine and there was a more masculine feeling to it. It smelt like him too, I breathed it in and realised how accustomed I've become to him.

Jake was humming an unfamiliar tune and I stepped closer and closer listening to him. His voice was like velvet and with every step towards the bathroom door I became more and more confident. I pushed the door open and clear as day there he was. All pure male and solid muscle drenched with water that sprayed across his toned body, I stared as each muscle flexed with his movement.

It was as though the he was sculpted by the Greek gods and they wanted one perfect human to roam the earth. How very, very nice of them.

I kicked off my flip flops and quickly disposed of my clothing and bikini then stepped forward to open the glass door.

"Mind if I join you?"

Jake's POV

I stood in the shower letting the powerful spray ease my stiff shoulders. I fought the images of our little tryst on the plane and instead tried to think of all the work that would be waiting for me when I got back home. I heard a click but didn't think anything of it, probably just the trees hitting the window or something.

"Mind if I join you?" a husky voice asked. A slow smile made its way onto my lips and I refused to fight the images any longer. I turned to face a naked Sasha and I heart raced, she really was so beautiful. The only thing she wore was a grin on her face and although she acted confident I could see the hesitation in her eyes.

"Not at all" I replied with a smirk. I held a hand out to her and she gripped it with her small one before stepping inside the shower. Immediately the water hit her skin and I watched the rivers of water cascade down her luscious body.

"The water is colder than I thought" she giggled and my eyes sought her nipples. They were standing erect in the perfect position for suckling. I chuckled.

"Yes, I had to try to cool my body down, but that doesn't look like it's going to happen. You already look like you've been cleaned from our flight here but since you're being such a dirty girl I might have to wash you clean" I winked at her and her eyes dilated and darkened at my teasing.

"Uh, uh, uh... this is my show. My experiment, therefore I make you feel good... before we both feel good." She leaned around me, giving me a peek at her globes behind her, and squeezed some shower gel on her hands.

She started at my shoulders, rubbing my knots away before sliding her hands down my arms leaving a trail of bubbles. Gliding them back up the inside of my arms she landed on my chest. She pushed me. Not hard but enough to make me stumble a little and hit the wall behind me and she continued rubbing my chest in circular motions slowly heading south to my abs.

She cleaned each one more than I could bear and just as she was nearing exactly where I wanted her she bypassed my throbbing erection and washed down my legs. She rubbed her expert hands up the back of my legs and over my ass pulling me forward and grinding me against her mound. I groaned at her teasing and tried to ease myself inside of her. But she wouldn't have any of it.

"I don't think so lover." She whispered teasingly and smoothed her hands around my back softly letting her finger-tips caress the skin of my back.

"Don't tease me Sasha, that's not very nice of you" I growled. But all she did was smile and fluttered her long eyelashes.

Gently, oh so gently, her fingertips grazed around and lower heading closer and closer to my sex. I was pretty much panting by now and couldn't wait to feel her touch. With a finger she started at the bottom of my balls and slid it up to twirl around the tip of my erection. It twitched with finally getting some attention and I gulped, I couldn't take much longer.

"You might want to hurry up or you'll make me explode soon baby" I whispered.

She obviously heard me because she grabbed me with both her hands and began to pump; up, down, up, down, up, down. It was pure pleasure and I was moaning at the feel of her small hands on me.

Water washed the soap off my body and she knelt down and immediately took my whole length into her mouth. She pumped her mouth, deep throating me over and over. I could feel myself hitting the back of her throat and I could feel the familiar tensing begin.

"No!" I gasped. She looked up at me totally confused and surprised.

"Did I do something wrong?" she gasped back breathing heavily.

"No! God hell no! You were, you are perfect. But... I'm not going to finish now." I replied. Before she could comprehend what I had in mind I walked her backwards until she was the one against the shower wall.

"My turn" I whispered into her ear before bending my head to take her nipple into my mouth. I swirled around with my tongue and bit it gently, rolling it between my teeth. She arched her back and pushed more tantalizing flesh into my mouth. I moved to the mound of her breasts and sucked hard on the skin leaving a fresh dark mark. My souvenir.

Sasha's POV

I shouldn't have tortured him so much. I should've known that he would have done the same to me and here we are. I was so close to begging him, I needed the pressure between my thighs to ease and he was avoiding my area so damn well.

My body was covered with bubbles and when he was finally satisfied he turned around and detached the shower head. Oh Lordy.

"This is for being such a dirty girl, my Sasha" he said before spraying every bubble of soap from me. He sprayed the bubbles from my breasts and followed it by sucking and licking my nipples then down my stomach.

He kneeled down and used the shower head to wash down my legs then slowly began his journey up the inside of my thighs, oh God he was so close to the apex of my legs, I was becoming so wet and it had nothing to do with the shower. He stopped just close enough that the little sprays were hitting my core, but it wasn't close enough to satisfy me.

"Oh God Jake, please!" I cried trying to get closer to the powerful spray but he kept moving it away.

He smiled then aimed the shower head straight at my core and I gasped. It was such a different feeling. It felt oh so good but just not enough.

As if reading my thoughts, Jake slid two fingers in and begins his torture all over again. As it was, I was gasping with ragged breaths from the sensations of the shower head and his magical fingers but then he joins them by kissing and sucking the inside of my thighs. I couldn't handle it and soon my walls were grabbing at his fingers, tightening and throbbing.

Jake dropped the shower head and joined his fingers with his tongue and that was I needed to explode with his mouth clamped around me. I screamed as my orgasm took over my body and my hips convulsed. During my climax Jake grabbed my ass and pulled me closer to his mouth sucking my juices from me, prolonging my orgasm until I had no strength left in me.

Holy shit!

"Holy shit!" I repeated out loud. I was gasping for breath, that was the most amazing orgasm I'd ever had, and by far the most powerful!

"Oh baby, we're not done yet" he gasped into my ear, copying my words from the plane. He spun me around and placed my hands on the wall. "Don't move."

He used his foot to separate mine and moved his hands to caress my breasts, pinching and rolling my nipples around again. I could feel him sliding his huge throbbing cock over my swollen bud and I whimpered at the tingles it sent around my core.

All of a sudden he plunged into me from behind and slammed into me hard and fast, and getting even harder and faster as he went. I was screaming in pleasure and it echoed around us in the bathroom, then suddenly I climaxed again and again and again. He wrapped his arms around my torso for support and with one last thrust he groaned my name and let his orgasm take over as he released his hot seed deep inside me.

"Oh my God... Jake that was... that was just amazing! Amazing doesn't even cover it!" I gasped with trembling knees.

"Tell me about it. You nearly killed me with your sexy body." He gasped back. "Let's get of the shower before we either fall or die from hyperthermia."

I didn't notice until he told me, but the water was freezing now. I guess he heated me up so much that I hadn't felt it earlier. He scooped me up bridal style and stepped out of the shower before putting me on my feet. He grabbed a fresh towel and dried me down, very thoroughly I might add. I did the same to him and I noticed he was aroused again.

"Somebody's a little excited again" I joked eyeing his growing arousal. He chuckled and shrugged his shoulders.

"Sorry, just looking at you and touching your body sends me in overdrive. You're just too sexy for your own good Sasha." I laughed and shook my head.

"I was thinking just the same thing about you actually"

Then to show him what I meant I grabbed his hand and pulled him to the bed where I showed him just how sexy I found him.

After another round of exhausting sex we took another shower, separately, and met in the kitchen. He was already sitting at the counter with a beer in front of him and looked up when I entered. He held up an unopened beer and raised it towards me.

"Would you like one?" he asked. I nodded and he opened it before handing it to me.

"So where's this favourite part of the house you mentioned earlier?" I asked taking a gulp from the cool beer.

"It's around this way, would you like to finish your beer first or walk and drink?"

"Let's walk and drink" I offered, and we jumped off the high chairs and I followed him towards the back of the house.

He opened a sliding door that I hadn't noticed before and waved a hand for me to go through first. He closed the door and grabbed my hand pulling me forwards. As we rounded the house I saw that his house was actually by the beach.

How the hell did I not notice that? I must really be getting distracted by him if I didn't notice that. It was beautiful though; white powder sand with crystal blue water that darkened at the deeper areas. I noticed that there weren't waves close to the shore and I raised an eye brow.

"How come the waves stop at the back?" I asked noticing that there were waves lapping a few hundred feet away but then stop making the water closer to the shore completely still.

"The waves stop because there is a reef over there that stop the waves, then as you can see all the area close to us is like a natural pool and is always the perfect temperature. I wanted to know if you wanted to go snorkelling later and check out the reef?" he explained.

"Oh yes! I would love that. I've never been snorkelling before. The closest I've been snorkelling is probably the underwater screen saver on my computer" I joked.

He laughed and I couldn't help but admire the way his lips formed the perfect smile and his laugh was so carefree and contagious. I shook myself, I needed to get my head together if I wanted to execute this experiment properly.

We walked along the beach drinking our beers and chatting about platonic things before my stomach growled.

"Come on, let's go back inside and I'll fix us something to eat" he offered.

"What? The great Jacob Stone knows how to cook as well? You really do have no flaws do you?" I laughed.

"Oh what can I say, I guess I was just blessed" he sighed sarcastically. I laughed at him and he joined in, I was having way too fun with him.

For lunch I tried to offer Jake some help but he plainly refused and ordered me to take a seat and relax. I wasn't used to having him do things for me when I was always the one to run around and take orders from him. But I accepted what he wanted and watched him work.

He was fixing us a few different sandwiches, and due to the heat I'm sure anything heavier would made me feel sick. We ate in comfortable silence and I had to admit, the man knew how to put a sandwich together.

"So, besides snorkelling what else is there to do on this island of yours?" I asked curiously.

He swallowed the last bite of his sandwich and gulped some water before answering. "Hmm, well there's hiking, swimming, there's a cave further north that we could explore and there's always island hopping." He listed one after one.

"Island hopping?"

"Yes, there are several other islands close by as well as the bigger main one with the clubs and restaurants and a few shops. The other islands have markets and one even has an underwater petting zoo type of thing."

With everything he told me I started getting more and more excited. I mean seriously, an underwater petting zoo? That's awesome!

"We can definitely do all those things during our stay here, if you like?"

"Well, what would you like?" I countered him.

"I don't really mind. I'm usually here alone and just relax around the house, hike or go swimming, so if you wanted to go anywhere or everywhere it could be a first for me to." He shrugged.

"I would love to do all of them if we could" I said softly. I was torn because I'd never experienced this before and might not ever have the chance to do it again; on the other hand, I was here to pleasure Jake.

But he did say he hadn't done most of those things so I'm sure I can incorporate my experiment into it all. I smiled, this was going to be way too much fun.

6

CHAPTER 6

I swung lazily in the blue and green cotton hammock with my eyes closed just basking in the chilled atmosphere that Jake's island effortlessly provided. After we finished our lunches Jake suggested I take a nap during this time of the day. The heat was intense and I could only be happy that there wasn't much humidity.

Jake opted to sleep in his room with the air conditioner blasting away but I preferred the natural breeze and fresh air. I stumbled across the hammock while I walked around the house, I hadn't seen it earlier because it was situated on the side of the house closer to the beach instead of the front. I loved it, I so needed to buy me a hammock when we go back home.

I didn't really feel sleepy, just lazy. I grabbed a romance novel from my luggage, slipped off my top so I was just in my bikini top and short shorts and lounged on the hammock with a leg hanging out to keep my swinging going.

I loved romance novels. Not only were they highly beneficial for my experiment but I loved how the authors wrote the seduction and how they managed to suck you right into the story making you feel what their characters feel.

In this particular chapter the woman was being seduced by her love interest in a lighthouse. He'd finally succeeded in his seduction and was taking her against the windows letting their thrusting bodies be seen by everyone whenever the light flashed by.

I was getting hot, and that was a mixture between the heat of the island and the hotness of their lovemaking. That's what I wanted... I wanted crazy, spontaneous sex where people might be able to catch us or hear us. I wanted to feel like a teenager again and have the thrill of feeling something new.

I sighed. Yeah, I was only twenty-four years old but that was getting closer and closer to thirty, then forty, then fifty, then sixty and I really just wanted to get my non-career life going since I was happy with my career. I wanted to be able to connect with my children and not feel too old to keep up with them.

Oh well, this is what I'm here for, to sharpen my seduction and sex techniques and make sure that the man I'm with has his mind blown, among other things.

"You look like you were made for a place like this" Jake's deep voice commented.

I smiled to myself and turned to look at him. He was shirtless, his glorious chest on show just for me, and in a pair of black gym shorts, his hair was a little ruffled and he had a faint sleep line from his pillow across his cheek.

"Mmm, I wish. If I could, I'd live here forever. It's absolutely perfect here" I replied still lightly kicking the floorboards to keep my gentle swing going.

"Me too, but I'd get too lonely here. So it's a good thing you're here to keep me entertained" he winked with his cheeky smirk back on his face, "Would you like to keep resting or would you like to go snorkelling by the reefs?"

I bolted up with a huge grin plastered on my face and jumped off. "Oh, I'd love to go snorkelling!" I cried.

"Then I'll grab the masks and stuff and meet you at the back" he turned to leave and I stood for a few more seconds just staring at his ass of perfection. I shook my head and went to my room to grab a towel and slap on more sunblock.

"Does this mask make me look fat?" I joked pulling a weird face when he turned around to look at me. He laughed and shook his head and dove under the water.

I followed after him and the scene before me too my breath away. Underwater was like a whole new different world full of colours and different creatures. Corals and shells ranged from off white to pink to orange and everything between. I smiled when I saw the tiny little fish darting in and out of the coral and anemone and I continued to follow them as though they were my underwater tour guide.

Jake swam next to me and together we explored the living city surrounding us. I looked farther ahead where the water turned dark blue and saw that the sand dipped deeply. The sand beneath us had been the same depth since the shore since the waves weren't pushing it around so I was surprised to see that in the dark blue water there was a shark looming there.

I gasped and rose to the surface.

"Is everything ok Sasha?" Jake asked worriedly when he took a breath.

"There's a shark over there! We need to get out!" I cried starting to head back to the dry sand. However, I stopped when I head Jake chuckling and turned to face him.

"Those are black tipped sharks Sash, they won't hurt you unless you antagonise them. They're mostly harmless."

"Are you sure? Because I refuse to be responsible if you lose a limb."

"I'm positive baby" he planted a chaste kiss on my forehead and ducked underwater again to continue snorkelling. I felt a teensy bit nervous but I trusted him, besides he's been here for a long time so he'd know."

We continued snorkelling then I told Jake that I'd head back to shore and keep my tan on so he kept going while I laid my towel down and went to lie on top of it. Hmm, well it is a private island... the only people here are me and Jake. I grinned then undid the knots of my bikini before lying down my back to even out my goodies, I'd swap to my back in a few minutes . Topless sunbaking, here's another first for me.

Jake's POV

I'd always loved snorkelling. I went everytime I came here and the scenery was never the same. It always changed and yet was always beautiful and spectacular. I snorkelled for another ten minutes before finding it not as exciting without Sasha so I decided to join her.

I swam back and tore the mask off my face before searching for my sexy little seductress. I spotted her a few feet away half in the shade of a palm tree and my eyes widened. She was topless! I scolded myself to settle down, I'm not a crazy teenage hormonal boy.

She was lying on her stomach and had her arms by her side, her bikini top in a pile next to her head. I made my way to her and saw that she'd fallen asleep, it's a good thing she was partially under the shade otherwise she'd have some painful sunburn.

I grew hard as I watched a bead of sweat travel from the nape of her neck down her spine and soak into her bikini bottoms. I wished it was my tongue that was travelling down her body tasting the saltiness of her skin and her warm flesh.

I couldn't hold back. I dumped the masks in the sand and kneeled over her ankles facing her back so her legs trapped, but weren't touching me. I smoothed my hands over her skin caressing her tones calves and up to her thighs. She moaned but didn't stir so I continued my journey.

I gulped as I passed her core, leaving the best for last, and slid my hands up the sides of her womanly hips. Her head, which was resting on her arms, switched sides but otherwise didn't wake up and I rubbed little circles with my thumbs up the sides of her spine feeling little knots and gently easing them away.

I was hard now and I fought the urge to wake her up by slamming into her and controlled myself, letting her have an interesting wake up. As my hands reached her shoulders I let them fall to her side, feeling the soft roundness that poked from underneath her. I swallowed and also wished that she'd been facing the other way so that he could cup her soft mounds. But that could always come later.

My hands slid down her sides and met as I cupped her ass. God she had an ass to die for. I never understood the way women asked 'does my ass look big in this?' and force the man to say no because I loved a woman with curves. I loved the feeling of having those curves bounce back to me as I pumped into them and actually had something to hold onto besides hip bones.

Sasha had an amazing body. Curvy and not too skinny but magnificently toned. I circled my thumbs over each ass cheek causing her to moan again. I bent down and moved her bikini bottom to one side as I used the tip of my tongue to lick up her centre.

Her taste mixed with the sea was addictive and I had to have more. I carefully spread her legs and slowly licked her core from top to bottom sucking on her clit. Her legs twitched as I dipped my tongue into her juices that were flowing for my taking and her head bolted upright.

"What the…? Jake?" her sleep filled voice murmured.

"Yeah baby, just lie back and relax. I need to taste you so badly I couldn't wait and I didn't want to wake you." I muttered back letting my lips graze across her clit as I spoke and blowing little breaths of air across it.

"Oh God, Jake! This is by far the best way to wake up. I'll have to return the favour when you least expect it." She sighed and dropped her head back on her arms and spread her legs more for easier access.

I hooked my thumbs on the sides of her bottoms and pulled her swimsuit down her long legs. Now she was gloriously naked and damn did I want her like this all the time. I should definitely make our stay on the island have a ban on clothes!

I spread her lips and used my whole tongue to lick up her juices, her taste really was sensational and I drank her up. I twirled my tongue around her clit and dipped it in her channel again and began thrusting it inside of her making her moan and dig her hands in the sand.

Her ass was rising off the towel and I used my hands to keep her down. With two fingers I circled around her core and dip submerged my fingers in her hot channel with her rotation. She was moaning my name and I decided to end her torture. I plunged my fingers in thrusting it deeply inside and making circular motions.

She started panting heavily and groaned. Her hitching breaths encouraged me and I zoned onto her clit as I thrust my fingers in and out stroking her bundle of nerves inside. Her walls began to tighten and her toes were starting to curl then she cried out my name in ecstasy as she climaxed.

I greedily sucked her and drank her dry not wanting to waste a drop of it.

"God, you taste amazing." I mumbled against her lips as she arched her back.

Sasha's POV

I panted as my body attempted to collect itself after the most amazing orgasm on the face of the planet! He squeezed my ass cheeks and bent to bite one roughly. I squealed and attempted to pull away but he held me down as he proceeded to suck and create a huge hickey on my cheek.

"Jake! I've already got a hickey from you!" I giggled thrashing my naked body away from him.

"I'm just marking my territory Sasha" he grinned slapping my ass, ""You seriously have the most delectable ass Sasha. I could just bite it all day."

I slowly turned over so that my breasts were on display and his eyes narrowed onto them. He crawled up and I could feel his erection grazing across my flesh through his trunks. He dipped his head and rolled a nipple with just his lips darting his tongue out to wet the tip.

I moaned his name. How can he never cease to amaze me? His ability to set my body on fire was effortless! I brought my legs up and dragged his trunks down his body with my feet that that his glorious body was naked above mine.

He feasted and feasted on my breasts, bringing me closer to another orgasm and I was so wet there was no way he couldn't tell. His erection prodded against my core and I grabbed it. I pumped him slowly letting my thumb caress the tip of his erection with every up-stroke. He moaned and buried his face in my neck, his gasps feathering little breaths across my sensitive spot below my ear.

Suddenly I stopped stroking him and swapped it for rubbing circles around my clit. I was already wet but with his throbbing cock rubbing against it, I was literally dripping my juices over him and down my legs.

He groaned louder and grinded himself against me but letting me control him. I grinned, I loved to feel in control and knowing that I'm making him feel this way is so hypnotizing.

"Do you want it?" I whispered in his ear.

"Yes!" he choked out as I guided his cock to my core.

"How much do you want it?" I asked licking the shelf of his ear.

"Too much! Too much I might not even be able to make it inside of you!" Oh that was hot. It'd been a while since I felt so wanted like he made me feel, and I was fast becoming addicted to his words of pleasure.

He was still on top of me and I could feel his beads of sweat running down his back, and I could tell he was trying so hard not to shove himself in. I let the head of his erection push inside before pulling out and grinned when he cried in protest.

"Sasha! That's not fair!" he whined. I giggled.

I thrust upwards slowly enveloping him in my slick channel slowly and I could feel his hands gripping into my hair and pulling it with every slow second that I brought him into me. A pattern was created; slide an inch in, I moan and he grunts as he crushes himself closer to me and then repeat

Finally he was completely wrapped inside my body and we let out a breath.

"Make yourself feel good baby, do what you want with me" I whispered into his ear and he moaned deeply and I felt his cock twitch inside me.

I was in the air and I gasped that he lifted us up, our bodies still in contact.

"Jake what are you doing?!" I screamed wrapping my arms around his neck.

"Making myself feel good" was all I heard before my back was pushed against the palm tree behind us and he began thrusting upwards. Our bodies slammed together, the different feeling between the scratching of the tree to the slick rubbing of Jake's body was making my blood heat up and my body shiver.

"Oh my God, Jake! Yes! Holy shit right there, right there...right... THERE!" I screamed as I climaxed squeezing my thighs around his waist. He came too, shouting my name and grinding his hips against mine spilling his release into me.

We laid side by side, on our towels in the shade of the palm tree, still naked from our coupling. I didn't feel shy at all being in my birthday suit around him anymore. He knew my body inside and outside very, very well and I could say the same about him too.

I peeked at him from behind my shades and just marvelled at his perfection. Sweat was scattered over his chest and I found myself loving this look on him. My eyes travelled down his abs to his, now, soft package. I sighed, he was magnificent at sex. My body craved him, craved his touch, kiss and everything in between.

I was getting myself hot and bothered again. Surely he must be exhausted! I needed to cool down.

"I'm going to go for a swim" I said before quickly standing up and heading for the clear water. I stepped in and submerged myself in the perfect liquid.

I swam back and forth revelling in the feeling of the water slithering across my naked body and soon settled for lying down half in the water and half on the wet sand. It felt wonderful having the water lick around my legs cooling down my body from my way-too-hot thoughts.

"Are you ready for round two?"

I opened my eyes to the sight of Jake's erect cock and I grinned evilly. Oh he was too much!

I answered him by massaging his sacs and trailing my open lips up his hard erection.

"Oh yeah baby" I heard him say.

I continued licking and sucking him, stroking him while deep throating and soon he moved away to lean over me and without saying anything he pushed inside me. There was nothing slow about this seduction and no foreplay at all. We didn't need it because our bodies were already excruciatingly hot for each other.

The small waves lapped at our bodies, kissing between my legs as he thrusted into me over and over again. His hands gripped mine and held them above my head as he zeroed down to my nipples. It was amazing to feel the ocean water, his body and his tongue on me all at once and I exploded!

He slowed down and circled his hips making my orgasm last longer. When my walls loosened around him he started all over again pounding our hips together, the slapping sound of our wet skin the only sound I could hear.

"Oh God, I'm going to cum" he groaned as he pounded into me furiously. I clenched my teeth as I climaxed over and over and he cried out as he joined me into heavenly bliss.

"I seriously can't get enough of your body Sasha, you're something else" he gasped between breaths then picked me up to lay us down on the towels where we fell asleep in shade of the trees.

7

CHAPTER 7

"Would you like a drink?" Jake called out to me from the kitchen.

"Sure" I called back.

"What would you like?" he asked me and I really didn't care what drink I had.

"Surprise me" I yelled to him and settled back into the sofa of the cottage.

After our sex marathon and naps on the beach we headed back to his cottage and I made dinner since it had already gotten dark and now I was relaxing on the sofa waiting for him to give me some company. It was only our first day here and I was getting a nice tan all over my body, no tan lines for me I chuckled to myself.

"What's funny baby?" I hear Jake ask behind me. I shook my head and waved my hand to say 'oh nothing'. He was carrying a martini glass with a lychee in a clear liquid and a beer bottle. "For you" he said offering me the martini glass.

"What is it?" I ask him sniffing the drink. It smelt delicious!

"It's a lychee martini, I thought you might like it" he smiled. I returned his smile and took a sip of the drink and moaned. Oh my God it was so yummy and refreshing! I ended up pretty much sculling the rest of it.

"Whoa! Slow down there, beautiful" he cried laughing, "It might not taste like it, but that does have a fair bit of alcohol in it."

I just giggled and tilted the glass letting the lychee slide into my mouth and chewed on the cold fruit. I snuggled against him and faced the tv, even though I wasn't really watching it. It felt so right being here with Jake. It felt so effortless.

I found myself wishing that my future husband and I had the same kind of effortless relationship that Jake and I had with each other. I looked up him as he took another swig of his beer and watched his throat convulse as he swallowed. Somehow even that was sexy as hell!

I could feel myself heating up and I mentally shook myself. How the hell could he make me so horny without even trying! I might end up killing the guy from sexual exhaustion! I needed to get away from his intoxicating sexiness and stood up.

"I think I might turn in" I said. His face held a pleading expression that I didn't understand so I offered him a smile and kissed his cheek before turning and nearly running to my room.

"Goodnight Sasha" I heard him call out huskily before I closed my door.

Jake's POV

I didn't know what it was about Sasha but there was something about her that made me stiff all the bloody time! I tried to concentrate on the tv while she cuddled into my arm. Was she meaning to press her breasts against me or not? Because either way it was driving my hormones crazy!

I took another drink of my beer trying to cover her invigorating scent with the stench of my beer.

"I think I might turn in" I hear her say. I turn to look at her and found myself getting lost in her eyes. She had beautiful eyes that I could just explore forever and never get bored. She smiled and placed a chaste kiss on my cheek before turning around towards the hallway.

Shit! Say something! Say SOMETHING! Open your mouth and try to at least cough out something out!

"Goodnight Sasha" I managed to choke out before hearing the door close.

Nice...

I sighed and drank the rest of my beer. Usually I find comfort being here all alone, but now it just seems plain lonely and way too quiet for my liking. It was almost as though having Sasha around brightened any room like the sun immerging from behind rain clouds.

"Urgh!" I groaned. Well there was no point in staying here if I couldn't be with Sasha. I switched off the tv and made my way to my room. While passing Sasha's room I hesitated, wanting to knock and ask her to sleep in my bed with me, but forced myself to keep moving.

I stripped off my clothes and stepped into the shower turning the water on hot. Steam filled the bathroom in no time and I just left my forehead against the cool tiles willing myself to get a fucking grip!

I'd known Sasha for years! Even before she started working for me she'd been friends with Jenna for years and always had sleep overs and come on outings with us. So why the hell is she stuck on my mind now like super glue?

Without my permission my mind pictured Sasha. Her big emerald eyes framed by long dark eyelashes, her perfect nose and soft pouty lips. I paused my brain on the image of her lips and memories of what they could do on my body instantly made my dick stand on end.

I pressed 'play' on my mental remote and I could see the slope of her neck, her perfect breasts and taut stomach centred on her womanly hips that I loved.

I gulped and my hand automatically grabbed my erection, pumping it to the mental images of Sasha's sexy body. I could now imagine her delicious pussy that was situated right above her skyscraper legs. Mmm, her legs could last forever!

Now I visualized myself, naked, between those legs and sliding my hard cock into her wet pussy thrusting in and out over and over and over again. I pumped my hand around my erection quicker and imagined it was Sasha's channel squeezing me. Just as Sasha and I climaxed in my imagination I felt the familiar warmth spreading in my lower stomach and I came.

"Damnit... what the hell have I gotten myself into?" I mumbled to myself as the shower washed away any clues of what I was up to.

Sasha's POV

I couldn't sleep.

Even with the air conditioner blasting away I couldn't find myself comfortable and it had everything to do with my dirty thoughts instead of the comfortable bed. I sighed. I needed him. I needed his body on me, in me, around me or squashing me for all I care... as long as it was near me.

I threw the sheets off and slipped off the bed. I crept to Jake's room and knocked quietly. There was no light coming through the bottom. I pressed my ear to the door, nope, can't hear anything. I should just go... Just go back to my room and force myself to sleep even if I had to knock myself out.

But I didn't.

I turned the door knob and felt the cool air from the room burst through the open door way. I jumped through and quietly closed the door. The moonlight streamed through the uncovered window and highlighted everything in the room. Jake was sleeping in the middle of his bed on his back, completely oblivious to me.

I picked the sheet up and carefully got in. Immediately his amazing scent washed over me, giving me a sense of comfort and in no time I fell fast asleep.

I woke up feeling the warm sun against my skin. I looked around and remembered I snuck into Jake's room last night. He was still sleeping on his back and looked absolutely adorable while he slept. His mouth was slightly open and his bottom lip would wobble every time he breathed. He looked so innocent.

The sheet had slipped down just past his hips leaving his naked torso completely on show, yummy! I licked my lips and felt myself get wet at the sight of his perfectly chiselled body. Time for some payback I think.

I grinned evilly and pulled the sheet off careful not to wake him. I began to massage him through his shorts and his erection was quick to stand. I watched his face as I carefully pulled his shorts down and stopped everytime he moved.

Finally I got them off and moaned at his rod standing up proud. God I need that inside me!

I crawled between his legs, thinking that this man slept like a bloody rock, and dipped my head. Slowly and lightly using the tip of my tongue I licked the bottom of his sacs and dragged my tongue over them to the base of his erection and licked up all the way to the tip.

I circled the head and sucked when I saw a drop of precome bead itself on the tip. Jake moaned loudly and raised his hips. I smiled and slowly brought my mouth down taking inch by inch of his throbbing cock.

I began to pump my mouth up and down while caressing the base of his erection with my hands and started getting faster.

"Holy shit! Oh God Sasha! This is the fucking best way to wake up. Shiiiiit!" I heard Jake moan just as he woke up.

His hands flew to my hair brushing it to the side and he looked at me desperately sucking his cock. I kept eye contact with him and saw his pupils grow dark with lust. He grabbed fistfuls of my hairs and began to fuck my mouth.

"Holy shit your mouth feels fucking amazing" he groaned.

His dick was prodding against the back of my mouth and I was gasping with every thrust out of my mouth, then I took over again deep throating him and sucking hard.

"Fuck! I'm going to cum!" He cried pulling my hair making me get even wetter.

I sucked hard and felt his seed burst into my mouth. I sucked him dry still moving my mouth, pumping him gently.

After a few minutes I crawled up his body kissing his naked flesh until I could slump on top of him.

"Good morning Jake, I hope you don't mind me slipping in your bed in the middle of the night" I whispered in his ear.

"Very good morning to you beautiful! If that's how I get repaid then you can do anything you want" I laughed and bit his muscled chest. "So what did you want to do today? Though

I'm not going to reject you wanting to stay in bed" he joked winking down at me while playing with my nipple.

"Um… well, I don't really- really mind" I stuttered. His fingers were plucking at my nipple causing it to bead tightly at his touch. "How about we go for a hike and check out that cave you mentioned earlier?" I asked, trying to keep my head straight.

His hand moved to the other nipple and was sending shocks of pleasure from my nipples to my core and I swear my juices were dripping .

"Sure, we'll get to that later" Then he proceeded to bend his head and grasp my nipple with his teeth while licking over them. His erection was prodding against my core and I simply slipped it inside. I felt every inch fill me up and I arched up grabbing at the head rest before bouncing on top of him.

My breasts were swinging in his face and he reached up to cup them while thrusting upwards into me as well. He pressed my breasts together before grabbing my hips and lifting me up. I squealed at suddenly being lifted up as though I weigh nothing.

"Turn around baby girl" he said huskily.

He helped me sit back on him facing the other way so that I was reverse cowgirl-ing him.

"Now ride me baby, make yourself feel good and ride me as hard as you like" His words were so sexy and I grabbed his thighs as I grinded myself against his huge erection. I was moaning and crying in pleasure as his cock stroked my g-spot over and over. The pleasure as almost too much handle and I came quickly.

My walls tightened around him and I ground against him panting as my orgasm shook my entire boy.

"Now it's my turn" he whispered. He pushed me forwards bending me towards his thighs and he groaned. "Fuck Sasha! I love your ass! This is the sexiest view in the whole God damn world!" Then he was slamming into me. His cock was banging against my bundle of nerves and I couldn't stop climaxing!

I was nearly crying, completely overcome with pleasure, then just when I didn't think I could take anymore orgasms his hips bucked and he cried out name.

I had his thighs in a death grip and my whole body was shaking. I don't think I could even move, the pleasure was that intense. He seemed to have understood because he lifted me up and brought me to lie down next to him. He spooned me from behind and kissed my neck.

"I really don't know how many times I need to tell you this, but you're fucking amazing Sasha. I can't get enough of you. If it was up to me... you wouldn't be leaving this bed until we have to leave."

A few hours later and we finally got out of Jake's bed. The sun was well up in the sky and the island was alive with nature. I'd showered and dressed in a white singlet with white washed denim shorts and sneakers, we were going to go hiking through the forest to the cave and I was waiting for Jake to hurry up.

I sighed, he was taking forever!

"Ready to go?" he said popping out of nowhere. I laughed.

"Yeah, ages ago. I'm ready to take my flying car out for a spin." I joked.

"Yeah, yeah, yeah, I took a while I get it ha-ha." He smiled joking back, "But, I made us a picnic so we can eat when we reach the cave." He turned around and showed me the bulky back pack he had hiked up on his back.

"Ok, I forgive you now!"

We grabbed anything we needed and headed outside to start walking towards a dirt trail that'd lead us to the cave.

8

CHAPTER 8

The brown dirt crumbled under our footsteps as we walked up the dirt trail up the mountain. We chatted easily for a while then settled on a comfortable silence, letting the sounds of the wind, tropical birds and the scampering of hidden animals fill our ears. I gazed around amazed at the beauty surrounding me and breathed in the fresh air.

We'd been walking up the mountain, over boulders and rocks, for the last hour or so when I could hear the rushing of water. A small creek came into sight and I smiled at the sight of the fish swimming through the pebbles.

"Are you ready?" Jake asked. I furrowed my eyebrows wondering what he was on about.

"For what?" I asked back.

He winked instead of answering and grabbed hold of my hand. He pushed through the foliage and I gasped as a beautiful waterfall came into view. We stopped at the bank of the water and he dropped the bag he was carrying then rolled his shoulders. Exactly how rich is he?!

"Like it?"

"It's so beautiful" I whispered, not even looking at him but at the majestic waterfall in front of us.

I heard him chuckle and just when I was going to turn to look at him his shirt came flying into my face. I totally wasn't expecting that.

"What the hell?!" I cried dumping his shirt on the ground, it was all sweaty!

He was bursting out laughing but I couldn't help but stare at his perfect torso. Ok, fine, he wants to play it that way then let's play.

I smirked and pulled my shoes, socks and clothes off quickly followed by my bra and panties. Who was laughing now? I thought to myself.

Jake's POV

Oh.

My.

God.

I couldn't breathe. I'm not breathing. I'm pretty sure I will die any time now from not breathing.

Sasha was standing butt naked in front of me and I managed to quickly glance at her perfect body before she dived into the pool of water. I don't understand why I'm acting this way when I've already seen her naked so many times before.

"Well?! Are you coming in or not stud?" she called out after coming up.

"Is it cold?" I asked. If it's freezing there's no fucking way I'm getting in there.

"It's perfect Jake! Get your sexy ass in here! And don't be a girl... I want all your clothes in a pile right now!" she laughed.

I narrow my eyes at her and quickly dispose of my clothes then dived in after her.

HOLY SHIT!!! IT'S FUCKING FREEZING!!!

I kicked my way up from under water and gasped in the warm air.

"Shit!" I yelled, my skin was covered with goosebumps and I shivering like mad. "Sasha what the hell?! You said it was perfect?!"

She was doubling over in laughter and if I wasn't freezing my ass off I'd be taking in the sight of her beautiful smile. I swam over to her and wrapped my arms around her, damn she was just as cold as I was. Her lips were turning a pale blue and I could hear the slight chatter of her teeth.

Goosebumps were covering her naked flesh and I automatically began rubbing her arms up and down even though there was no way that could warm her up.

"Jesus Sash you're freezing!"

She shivered violently and cuddled up to me winding her arms around my waist and digging her fingernails into my back. "Care you warm me up then stud?" she whispered huskily into my ear.

I growled and dipped my head to capture her lips with mine. I bit her lower lip making her gasp and took the opportunity to slip my tongue inside her warm mouth. I could feel her nails digging into my back and her legs wound around my hips, tightening until my erection was trapped between us.

I couldn't help the moan that escaped my lips and I crushed her against my chest loving the feeling of her breasts pressing against me. I pressed her up by a rock on the bank and rubbed the head of my erection against her clit. I could feel her hot gasps of breaths warming my lips and I crushed my lips against hers again trying to warm her lips up even more.

Her hands roamed downwards to my ass and she clenched it pushing herself down onto my cock and I groaned out loud startling a few nearby birds as her hot channel took my whole length in. The contrast between the freezing water and her hot body were polar opposites and I wouldn't be surprised if we ended up turning the water into a bubbling jacuzzi!

She licked up the side of my neck and gently bit my earlobe and that was my undoing. I thrust upwards into her hitting the hilt gaining a loud gasp from her.

"Oh God Jake, I don't know how it gets better every time!" she screamed as I pounded into her, the water splashing around us and the waterfall crashing down behind.

Her walls tightened around me, squeezing the fucking hell out me more like it, and I roared as she screamed my name as she rode her orgasm milking me along with her. I thrust slowly letting our orgasms fade into oblivion and I could feel the pierced skin where her nails had gone through behind my shoulders.

"Oh my... oh... my... ahh!" she sighed. I could still feel her walls twitching from her climax and I was already hardening at the feel of it. I pulled out before I got ahead of myself and rammed into her again and again and again!

I bent and nipped her bottom lip while I caressed her waist just loving the feeling of her silky skin. She moaned and tried to deepened our kiss but I smirked and pulled back.

"Jakkeee!" she whined pulling the cutest pout and sticking out her bottom lip. I chuckled and pulled on her lip with my thumb and index finger while moving away trying to get a grip of my raging erection. She was like my own source of Viagra! It's like I couldn't ever get enough.

"Come on, I want to show you something" I told her.

I treaded water swimming backwards towards the waterfall while keeping my gaze on her. Her pupils were wide with lust and I could see her eyes roaming across my bare chest. She smirked and dove under the water giving me a view of her bare buttocks before her tiny feet disappeared under the water.

I laughed and turned to swim properly towards the waterfall. I was a fast swimmer so when I reached the rocks close to it I leaned against them and waited for Sasha to come up. I waited and waited but she didn't come up. I started to get worried until I saw a blurry figure float towards me. Sasha popped up from underwater right in front of me gliding her breasts up my chest. Damn her.

"Mmm, I like the view underwater" she whispered huskily.

And there's that raging boner again.

"You're a cheeky one, aren't you" I replied pecking her on the lips. "Come on, follow me"

I turned around towards the waterfall and used the smooth rocks to step on to walk behind the waterfall.

Sasha's POV

I watched him disappear behind the waterfall and gaped. What the hell? Where'd he go?

I followed him using the same rocks as he did and noticed the gap behind the rushing water. I entered behind it and found myself in a hidden cavern. There was minimal light but from what I could see it was small but spacious and the floor was completely smooth rock. The air smelt damp but not horrible.

"Wow this place is cool!!" I gasped hearing my voice echo off the walls. I mean, it was a cave... but how many people can honestly say they found a cave behind a waterfall void of creepy crawlies and bats?

"I found this place a while ago but this isn't all. Come on" he said taking hold of my hand. I didn't even find it awkward that we were walking through a cave completely naked.

He pulled me behind a large boulder that I didn't even notice I saw a narrow tunnel that lead to another cavern. We walked through to it and I gasped when I saw that the cave looked like there were thousands of fairy lights decorating the walls.

"What is this?" I asked Jake.

"They're glow worms. Beautiful aren't they?" he answered and I nodded vigorously. It was such an amazing sight and so beautiful.

We left the cave to gather the picnic things and carefully brought them back inside to the glow worm cave. While Jake laid a blanket down on the cold floor I slipped on my clothes and threw his at him. We ate the food he brought just gazing around at the glow worms and it was almost as though the midnight sky was inside with us.

"Thank you" I said quietly.

"For what?"

I looked at him. His face basked in the glow of the thousands of glowing bugs and I smiled.

"For showing me such a special place" I shrugged.

I stood up and sat on his lap with my knees on either side of him. I stroked the sides of his face and we just looked at each other's eyes before I bent my head and kissed him passionately. He'd been so accommodating and sweet I was in danger of falling in love with the man but I offered him no strings attached sex and that's what we both agreed on.

I felt him lie down on the blanket and stroke the length of my back while his erection poked me. I wanted to show him how much this meant to me without saying any such words so

I kissed down his bare chest, seeing as he didn't bother with a shirt, and sealed each kiss with a lick. I could hear each of his breaths becoming ragged and once again I felt like a powerful woman with the ability to make such a sexy and accomplished man like Jake react this way.

I slowly pulled his shorts down and gripped his rod kissing the tip. I swirled my tongue around the head before slowly bringing his whole length inside my mouth. I heard him moan and I continued to pump my mouth up and down while I massaged his sacs. He was so hard and I couldn't help myself from becoming wet.

I licked and sucked him over and over again pulling back or slowing down whenever he warned me he was close. I knew I was driving him crazy and to be honest I loved it. All of a sudden I felt myself being pulled up and the next thing I knew I was straddling him.

"No more teasing baby" Jake choked out before he pulled my shorts off and slid me onto him. He was oh so hard it felt like he was impaling me on him and I began stroking him with my pussy. I moved off my knees onto my feet so I was squatting over him and every down stroke felt even deeper!

"Holy shit!" he cried gripping harder into my hips. He moved his hands to my breasts and began pinching my nipples just enough to make me cry out and slam down onto him. I was sweating from the effort, my thighs were burning and yet I kept going because the sheer pleasure shooting between them straight into my core was bliss. This coupling wasn't like other times. I used my body to show him how much he was starting to make me feel.

How I already feel for him.

I leaned backwards using his thighs to keep me steady, arching my back, and began pumping harder when I could feel my climax building quickly. My breasts were poking out and my head swung back as I impaled myself down onto him and I screamed his name the same time he called mine. I circled my hips making our climax last longer and I could hear our screams fortified and echoing around the cave.

I slumped forward onto his chest and listened to his racing heart thud erratically. His arms circled around me and squeezed me tight, and to be honest I never wanted him to let me go. That was a bad sign.

"Fuck Sasha. I think you may have killed me and brought me to heaven" he panted heavily.

I smiled against his chest and a giggle escaped my lips. "I could say the same thing about you "

We stayed in the same position for a little while longer, me just listening to the beating of his heart, before a howling noise ricocheted around the cave. A huge gust of wind had managed to enter the cave and rushed through the tunnel.

"Well, we'd better go. It must be getting late already." Jake announced. I was sad to leave but I guess we could always come back if we wanted to. We gathered our things and left our dark hide out.

By the time we stepped out from behind the waterfall the sun was already getting low and were shooting rays of last sunlight through the gaps of the leaves.

Oh... well I'd hate to waste the romantic setting.

"Say Jake... did I ever mention that having sex with a mermaid was one of the most popular fantasies?"

9

CHAPTER 9

We spent the rest of the evening eating junk food to 'put on all the calories we lost' according to Jake. He had a serious sweet tooth and apparently had sweets hidden everywhere. We were currently sitting on the soft rug surrounded by wrappers of toffees and boxes of expensive chocolate.

"Ergh, I'm starting to feel sick" I groaned holding my still flat stomach.

"But we have so much more to eat babe" he replied walking to the kitchen.

I looked up at him and saw he was holding a tub of honeycomb ice-cream. Damn, where the hell does he put all this junk food?

"I don't think I can make it!" I cried.

"Aw, come on... just a little"

He sounded so seductive I almost forgot he was talking about ice-cream. I seriously needed to work off these calories. I eyed the bucket of ice-cream he was already digging into and a light bulb dinged in my head.

"I'm going to grab something to drink. I think you probably could make rocky road what's stuck in my teeth! Did you want something?" I asked.

"No thanks I'm good" he replied shovelling another spoonful into his mouth.

I grinned. He was too cute sometimes. I poured a large glass of water and popped in a lot of ice cubes to keep it freezing cold then went over to the pantry to grab whipped cream and chocolate syrup.

Jake had moved to the sofa now and called out that if I wanted some I'd have to hurry before he ate it all. So I quickly hurried out of the kitchen snapping off the lights. The TV illuminated our faces but the characters were in some sort of cave so there wasn't that much light anyway.

"You want some baby?" he asked me holding a spoon out to me. I shook my head and took a gulp of cold water keeping it in my mouth.

I slid down the sofa and caressed his manhood. He jumped in surprise and luckily for me so did another part of him. I massaged his sacs through the thin material of his shorts and I smiled when he put the bucket aside and moved my hair over my shoulder.

I pulled his shorts down carefully and his dick sprung out. He was fully erect and I nearly swallowed the freezing water at the sight of it. I could never get over seeing his impressive pole. I tilted my head back, keeping the water at the base of my throat and took his head into my mouth.

I swooped down and took his whole length. He gasped and groaned at the sudden change of temperature and his hands curled into my hair as I worked my mouth up and down. The water changed from freezing cold to lukewarm so I swallowed and he panted as the walls of my walls engulfed him.

"Jesus Christ Sasha! What the hell are you doing to me?!" he groaned loudly.

I sucked him hard, easing off, making a popping sound when he slipped out. I curled my tongue around the tip and his cock throbbed between my stroking hands.

"I have an idea to both lose and gain calories" I whispered.

"An-And what did you have in mind?" he gasped.

I was wearing his shirt with only panties underneath so I grabbed it and pulled it off. He moaned at my nakedness and his hand went towards my breast but I slapped it away.

"Uh, uh, uh... no touching" I dragged my breasts up his body. His cock glided between the valley of my breasts before sweeping down my stomach while I pressed my chest to his naked one. I brought my mouth to his earlobe and bit it softly tugging at it. "You wouldn't want me to tie you up for being naughty would you?"

"Holy shit! I'd much rather be the one doing the tying up" he whispered huskily back to me.

I straddled him causing his penis to poke my core through my already wet panties and leaned over to grab the whipped cream. His eyes widened and his pupils dilated as it followed my every move. I squeezed whipped cream onto my erect nipples and I shuddered at the coolness of it against my heated skin.

He leaned forward to lick it off but I pushed him back into the sofa and bounced on his dick swirling my hips around. He groaned out loud and pushed up but I lifted my hips to end contact with him.

"You don't touch unless I say so Mr Stone" I said strictly. He smirked and leaned backwards watching me intently. I picked up the chocolate syrup and messily squirted it over my nipples, then breasts with some landing on his chest.

"Oops... I got some on you" I apologised coyly before bending to slowly lick it off. He was stiff as a board and felt as though he'd break my panties any time now.

"Sasha...-"

"That's Miss Montgomery, Mr Stone" I interrupted him.

"Miss Montgomery... please!" he gasped.

I pushed forward and held my sweetened breasts in front of him as he ravaged me. He licked the whipped cream off and sucked my chocolate nipples until I was all clean. He bent his head and began on the underside of my breasts gliding his tongue over the swells before heading back to my nipples.

"Slow down Mr Stone, I have much more planned for you" I said coyly. I slid off his lap and pulled my panties off before walking down to his bedroom making sure to bring the chocolate syrup and whipped cream. "Follow me"

I barely stepped into his bedroom when I heard him scrambling forward and barge into the room. I held a hand in front of me to stop him coming closer and pointed to his large bed. He slid over the covers and laid on his back with his arms behind his head. His cock twitched with excitement but his eyes roamed over my body attentively. I pulled out four colourful scarves and threaded them through my fingers feeling the smooth silkiness of them.

"So what do you have in store for me Miss Montgomery?" he asked.

I held the scarves with two hands and swayed my hips as I began to dance for him. I twirled and rocked my hips getting closer to him and tied one foot then the other before tying up his hands to the bars above him.

He was breathing heavily and I stepped up on to the bed continuing my dance. I stepped over his hips so each foot was either side of him and I bobbed my hips down spreading my legs to show him a glimpse of my wetness.

"Sash-Miss Montgomery, I can't wait too long!"

"Too bad Mr Stone, you'll have to"

I straddled him hovering just over his erection as I squirted more whipped cream and chocolate over his body and finally over his beautiful penis. I started at his nipples, ravaging him as he did me and following the trail of sweetness to his throbbing manhood. His hands pulled at his bonds as he tried to grab at me but the scarves held him back.

I licked the mountain of whipped cream before eating him. I sucked the sides of cock slurping the sugary treat from his salty skin before taking his whole length and pumping his entire cock with my hot mouth.

"Sasha!!!" Jake cried.

I was way past foreplay as well and I straddled him again holding his swollen tip to my dripping wet pussy. I rubbed his dick in circles over my engorged clit spreading my juices over my pussy then swiftly plunged him in deep. Very, very deep.

"Holy fuck yes!!!" He shouted before thrusting into me. I bounced down on him and rode him hard grinding my hips against his feeling him hit me deep inside.

My walls squeezed his engorged and throbbing erection and I threw my head back screaming his name as my climax exploded. It was like a chain of explosives going off one after another and I barely heard Jake cry out my name before he thrust upwards with excessive force and spilt himself inside me.

We both collapsed and breathed hard, our chests rising up and down as we tried to catch our breaths.

"Holy fuck! I've never really been into getting tied up but you sure as hell made it worth it" he panted loudly.

I just grinned seeing as I was totally unable to breathe.

"You know Miss Montgomery, I'd love to turn the tables on you. I'd love to tie you up while I squeezed chocolate all over your delicate skin. I'd lick every inch of you and make you scream my name countless times before I follow with my fingers and make you scream over and over again. Now untie me so I can make you beg"

I quickly undid his tight scarves and before I knew it he flipped me over to my stomach.

"But before I do just that, I'll need a little snack" he said and he thrust into me with yet another impressive and very hard erection. He pounded into me making my breasts grind into the sheets I was clutching while I screamed in pleasure.

"Come for me baby, and I'll spend the rest of the night making you come over and over again until you beg me to stop"

That did it. His furious mating and whispered words made me climax so hard the same time as him and I was like jelly.

He gently turned me over and carefully tied each limb so I was spread wide open. Unlike him, I was blindfolded which only heightened my sense of pleasure and I shivered as the chocolate syrup was squirted onto me.

He concentrated the syrup onto my nipples and my pussy and I waited with anticipation to feel his hot tongue to taste it. He started kissing my mouth, hot and passionate before he moved his expert mouth down my neck. He bit my shoulder making me shudder and then he began his licking.

His hot tongue swirled the chocolate, licking it all up and leaving a trail of saliva that cooled when he moved on. The mixture of hot tongue and cold air were sending goosebumps across my skin. He worked my nipples until they were straining for his mouth and all the while no other part of him touched me making me ache for more and more.

Slowly, oh so slowly, his tongue caressed the chocolaty skin of my taut stomach to my mound then he honed straight for my chocolate pussy. Melting chocolate dripped down across my clit to my core and he licked it all up dipping his clever tongue into my channel . His fingers joined him and by now I'd climaxed so many time I couldn't count!

"I need you" I whispered huskily and he obliged.

He pressed his cock to my pussy and played with the head of his dick, pushing in and out making me whimper. With one fast powerful thrust he entered me and pumped frantically into me. I took him all and wished I could hold him, cling onto him closer, but my thoughts were interrupted by more waves of pleasure.

He roared and came the same time as I did and thrust gently as his seed filled me.

"I think I'm becoming addicted to you Miss Montgomery" he gasped after untying me and holding me close.

I wanted to reply. I wanted to tell him I felt the same way, but I didn't know if he was talking about this facade or the real me.

10

CHAPTER 10

I was so stiff. I hadn't had so much sex in one day before but the stiffness with in places that made me smile and the things we did would've made me blush before. Jake and I ended up sleeping in my bed seeing as his was covered in chocolate and whipped cream and he was adorable when he slept.

I slowly rolled over to face him, my naked breasts crushing against his bare torso, and I watched him. His bottom lip fluttered with each intake of breath and a smile would creep onto the corner of his mouth every once in a while.

Jake was doing me a great favour by helping me with my experiment and if I was able to keep someone like him attracted to me without having wondering eyes then it would easy to stop my future husband from getting bored by me.

My heart ached at the thought of a future without this, Jake's warmth and humour and damn sexiness. I sighed, this was what I wanted. I began to wonder what would be the next fantasy I'd play forward for him, then the idea hit me.

Jake's POV

The smell of fresh coffee wafted to my nose and I grinned at the hominess it exuded. I could get used to this. I turned over to hug the beautiful woman next to me when I felt the empty space. The cold empty space.

Right, she was the one making coffee.

"Well good morning handsome" her sultry voice came.

I saw her leaning against the door frame in my shirt with her long bare legs poking out from the bottom. This is an image I wouldn't mind being burnt into my brain.

"Good morning, you look absolutely beautiful" I told her truthfully.

She ducked her head as she blushed and walked over to me.

"You know Jake, you're already going to get laid. You don't need to tell me those things" she said as she sat on the edge of the bed.

"It's the truth" I shrugged, "Besides I tell you because I want to not because I have to"

She smiled at me and I held her hand bringing her closer for a kiss. She tasted like coffee and jam and made me even hungrier for her taste. I deepened the kiss and I swallowed her moans. She pushed me backwards taking me by surprise and together we fell off the bottom of the bed.

Oomph!

"Shit, are you ok Sasha?"

She burst out laughing and buried her head in my chest making me join in with her.

"I made you coffee in the kitchen" she told me after our laughter died, I kissed her and stood up bringing her up with me. I could definitely get used to this.

"So what do you want to do today babe?" I asked her.

"Can we check out the other islands?"

"Sure, no problem. We can even stay at my friend's hotel if you want?"

Sasha's POV

Today was turning out even better than I thought. Jake was looking stunning in a white button down shirt with the sleeves rolled up and showing his sculpted chest and I changed into a yellow and white sun dress.

We'd shared a suitcase and took a speed boat to another one of the islands and were now waiting at his friend's hotel. Jake told me that we could stay for as long as we wanted here but I told him one night would be fine.

"Just this way Mr Stone" the bell boy directed us as he took our bags. "Mr Antonio has reserved only the best for you" he opened the door and I gasped at the beauty of the room. There was a king sized bed covered in white sheets threaded with gold which matched the colours of the room. A small chandelier hung above the room and threw the bright light around the room through the diamonds that hung from it.

There was a small closet and a large ensuite filled with the essentials and even a Jacuzzi, I got hot and bothered just imagining the things I could do with Jake there!

"Thank you... Simon" Jake thanked the bell boy handing him his tip and slapping his shoulder. He shut the door and pulled me to him immediately. "Are you having the same idea as me beautiful?"

He nibbled on my ear lobe and scratched his teeth on the sensitive spot just below sending shivers up and down my body. His hands slid down my body to grasp handfuls of my ass and he squeezed it pulling my mound to his hardening member.

Oh God! The familiar tingles of fireworks were spreading through my veins and I desperately needed to have a clear head if I was to keep my experiment going how I needed it. I couldn't lose myself to my feelings. I would end up getting hurt because Jake signed up for no strings attached sex. I had to remember that.

"Jake..."

"Mmm" he replied against my neck.

"Ja-Jake..." Damn, the things his mouth can do.

His mouth was trailing to my collarbone and sucking on my skin. As he got to the swell of my breasts I snapped to attention.

"Jake. Why don't we uh have a look around the hotel? Maybe check out the pool or something?" I was gasping and was so close to telling him not to stop. He heaved a sigh and rested his head on my breasts like a cushion.

"Okay, okay. You're just too damn sexy to resist" he told me before wrapping his arms around my waist and hugging me.

He was so warm and I fit so perfectly in his arms I wondered what it would be like to be Mrs Stone.

No! Sasha that is dangerous thinking!

"Let's go for a walk then"

"Um, you go down to the bar downstairs, I just want to change first. I'll meet you there in a few minutes" I smiled.

"Oh, okay" he pecked my lips and waved as he got to the door.

Alright, next fantasy coming up.

Jake's POV

I was waiting at the bar snacking on a bowl on nuts just counting the seconds for my sexy Sasha to come down. The hotel was classy yet had that casual beach feeling to it. Antonio had done well for himself. There were plenty of people enjoying a drink or having lunch , the bar was practically buzzing.

"Hey there stud, looking for a date?" a husky voice asked.

I turned to see a sexy woman wearing skyscraper high heels and a very short blood red halter dress with a neckline that scooped low to show off her assets. Her lips matched her dress and her eyes were framed with long dark eyelashes. It was quite obvious what her occupation was.

"No thank you" I told her looking away.

"Are you sure?" she urged circling her finger on my arm. I turned to look her straight in the eye to tell her to leave me alone when I stopped. Those eyes. This 'lady of the night' wore the same emerald green eyes as Sasha.

"Sasha?"

The woman winked at me and slipped onto the bar stool next to mine making her dress slide even further up her thighs. God damn.

"Did you know one of the most desired male fantasies is to have sex with a hooker? It almost ties with having an orgasm in public where anyone can catch you" she said matter-of-factly.

"Excuse ma'am, this is from the man at the end of the bar" the bar tender informed Sasha and he placed a martini in front of her. Blood boiled in my veins as I turned to see who the man who thought he had a right to buy my woman a drink.

Uh, my woman? I mean Sasha. I found a fairly good looking man younger than me with oily slicked back hair smiling at Sasha. When he caught my eye he smirked.

"Come on Sash-"

"Jacob! How are you doing?" a voice boomed.

I turned to the sound and offered a tight smile for Antonio. I was happy to see him but his timing couldn't be worse.

"I'm good Antonio, how have you been?"

Antonio spoke about how business was going but I couldn't pay attention. My attention was stuck on the woman who as being surrounded with male attention. There were several workers surrounding her as well the man who bought her a drink. She was laughing and sipping from her martini while the men couldn't keep their eyes off her body.

"Well, I see you have important business to attend to" Antonio chuckled as he caught here my gaze was. "I'll see you before you leave okay?"

I muttered a 'goodbye' and headed straight for Sasha.

"All ready to go sweetheart?" I announced loudly in front everyone.

"Sure" she smiled grabbing her purse and a small gift bag as she hopped off the stool. I threw a smirk at the men behind her back and left my hand on the small of her back leading her to a booth slightly hidden by large pot plants.

I know I didn't have the right to be jealous, but I'll be damned if I let anyone grab her from under my nose.

"I love it when you're all possessive Jake" Sasha whispered huskily in my ear. Her hand traced a path down my chest and dropped to land on my crotch. My eyes widened when she popped the button open and tried to unzip my pants.

"Sasha what are you doing?"

"My job" she told her staring straight into my eyes, "The name's Lola and you can be... John. It's my first day on the job and it's your first time with a hooker. You seem nervous so this will be on the house. If you want to know the prices, I can tell them to you after"

Holy shit! She was really getting into her role. I was stiff under her stroking hand and she began to kiss my neck as her hand began to unzip me again. She pulled the metal teeth apart and stuck her hand inside my boxers.

Her small hand was slightly cold making my cock jump at her touch.

"You're so big" she moaned as she began pumping me.

My eyes were in danger of closing and I was sure that, despite the table cloth hiding what was happening under the table, if I let the pleasure take over everyone would know.

I darted my gaze around the bar and she wasn't even holding back with her affection. Her thumb swirled over the tip of my swollen penis and I groaned shutting my eyes.

"Excuse me sir, is this lady bothering you?"

My eyes snapped open and landed on a man older than myself eyeing Sasha with distaste. Sasha stopped kissing me but continued to pump me letting her hand dip to caress my sac every now and then.

"The woman you're talking about is my wife, Mr...?" I trailed letting him fill me in on his name. Wife? What the hell?

"Oh uh, Thomas. Mr Thomas, I'm the manager here sir. I'm terribly sorry"

"Leave us be Mr Thomas" was all I growled before I threatened to have him fired. He scrambled away with a bright face and right now I couldn't care less. Sasha's hand was pumping faster and she was whispering seductive words into my ear.

"You better stop soon Sasha-"

"Lola. My name's Lola"

"Sasha. I'm going to burst soon if you don't stop! I'm serious, I'm so on edge right..."

I didn't have time to finish because she looked around before ducking under the table cloth and used her sweet, hot mouth to suck the come straight from my balls.

"Fuck!" I whisper yelled holding her head and thrusting gently into her mouth as I came streams into her sweet mouth. "Holy shit!"

Sasha was up next to me again after a few seconds and stroked my thigh.

"Let's walk, stud"

How could I say no?

Every pair of eyes followed us as we strolled through the hotel and the grounds. The hotel was by the beach which had spectacular white sand and crystal water which was full of families vacationing and singles wondering about or friends having fun.

We ended up by the pool and there were rows of sun loungers and little tents to change in that were each a different colour. The pool was huge, it was shaped like a river that disappeared behind a man-made island filled with palm trees.

"So what's in the bag?" I asked Sasha.

We stopped and she turned to me holding out the gift bag with a smile.

"It's just a little something for you from me, go and put it on" she answered pushing me towards the colourful tent.

Sasha's POV

I really wasn't enjoying the eyes that seemed permanently attached to my ass. I didn't think I would've minded so much because I loved it when Jake looked at me. With him I felt so comfortable with my body but I got shivers, and not good ones, when men's eyes followed me everywhere with their eyes raking all over my body.

Maybe this outfit wasn't the greatest idea.

Jake's head popped out of the tent with the curtain covering the rest of his body. "Sasha, I'm not going out wearing this"

I chuckled and walked into the tent. Jake was stark naked except for the tiny black spandex speedo I'd bought him. His wide shoulders made my knees weak and they tapered down to a smaller waist and a tight ass. Damn, damn, double damn.

"But John" I said using his role play name, "Don't you remember? My name is Lola, and besides if you wear that then I'll go out in this" I tell him slipping off my tight dress revealing the tiny white bathing suit underneath.

I could literally see his jaw drop as he stared at every inch of my body. "Then I'm not wearing it, because I don't want any other man seeing your sexy body. Only me"

I felt quite flattered at his gaze.

He walked to me and kissed my lips very lightly. His lips whispered over mine and a hint of tongue warmed my bottom lip. His fingertips slid down the side of my breasts and then he used his thumbs to circle my nipples through the thin bikini top.

"You're being very naughty Sash-"

"Lola. Call me Lola"

"Baby, I don't want to be with anyone else but my Sasha. So I'm calling you Sasha" he whispered against the shell of my ear. His whispered words were so erotic I could feel the pool of pleasure gathering between my thighs.

I need to be in control. Snap out of it!

"Let's go back to our room and I'll show you how much I want Sasha and not Lola. Let me kiss your neck and lick your nipples while I plunge into your core with my fingers and make you come one after the other. Just when you think I'm finished I'll stick my cock deep inside of you and make you scream my name" He whispered grinding his erection against my mound.

His words were enough to put me on the brink of climax but I needed to stop him before I forget what I was supposed to do!

"How about you show me that after we swim" and with that I ran and dived into the pool letting him see the back of my g-string bikini bottoms.

The cold water snapped my over heated brain back into reality. I heard a splash behind me and I started to swim away from him to collect my scattered thoughts a little more. I swam away from the hotel and just as I reached the underside of a little concrete bridge that arched over the pool Jake's warm rough hand grabbed my ankle and pulled me backwards.

We broke the air and I started laughing. "Shit you're a fast swimmer!"

"Only when I'm going after something I want"

His lips crashed on mine and he swam us to the edge of the pool, "I need you Sasha. Please don't push me away again"

Now there was no way in hell I was going to be able to.

His erection was hot and hard and pushing its way between my thighs. I was caged between his muscled arms and his lips were attacking mine as though he would die if he wasn't kissing me. I felt his fingers pull aside the material covering my mound and he dipped two fingers inside and began to pump.

I gasped and started moaning.

"Someone might see us Jake!" I whispered to him leaning my head backwards to rest of the concrete.

"I don't care. I need to have you Sasha!"

He pushed his throbbing member inside me and I moaned loudly at his heated skin rubbing against mine. His chest rubbed against my bouncing breasts and he began sucking on my neck as his pumping into me harder and harder. Our hips were grinding and the pleasure was building.

I was so close to orgasm!

Footsteps began walking over the bridge and Jake was thrusting so hard the water was splashing around us. My climax hit me and I bit into his shoulder to stop my screams of pleasure so no one would hear me.

"Fuck!" Jake swore as he thrust deep one last time and came after me making my orgasm last longer. He held my face and kissed me deeply and passionately before leaning his forehead against mine.

"I think I see the reason behind having sex where you might get caught" he panted.

CHAPTER 11

Jake's head lowered to my neck and his tongue poked out to trace heated circles from my jaw down to my collarbone and I was close to melting into a puddle. Despite the coldness of the water and the heat from our latest escapade I found myself needing him again.

I couldn't understand where all this hunger for his body came from. If I was like this with my previous partners then none of them would've cheated on me. I threaded my fingers through his raven hair and felt the thick strands tickle the side of each finger.

I bent my fingers and caught his thick hair pulling his head back so I could look into his deep chocolate eyes. They were darkened with lust and I just couldn't help myself. I smashed our lips together and bit his bottom lip as his hot tongue fought with mine.

I couldn't breathe!

I opened my eyes and saw that we slipped underwater in our haze of lust and I pulled back quickly kicking myself up to breathe fresh air. I saw his head break the surface of the water and watched as the drops of water rolled down the side of his face.

"Come on, let's get out of here before we actually do get caught" I joked as I swam up the pool. The pool circled around the man-made island and Jake and I lazily swam around talking and joking. Being with him felt so easy. I didn't have to over think my actions or find myself scrambling for something witty to say. I could just be me and he seemed to like it.

We were back to the main part of the pool and lazing about on the steps of the shallow pool. I sat on the steps leaning my elbows on the step behind me while his chin rested on my knees and the rest of his delicious body floated behind him.

A drop of water landed on my nose and I looked upwards to see the sky had grown to a dark grey and was spitting drops of rain.

"Scared of a little rain?" Jake teased.

"No, I actually really like rain. I always have since I was a little girl, it helped me sleep better" I replied truthfully. He smiled and kissed my knees.

I closed my eyes as I felt more and more cool rain drops fall and hit every part of my exposed skin. Soon thunder began to clap and lightening slashed through the sky as the wind picked up and howled around us.

"We should head back in Jake. I love the rain but I prefer it from somewhere warm and safe"

"Sure, let's go" he stood and I was momentarily frozen at the sight of his powerful body standing in front of me with sheets of water sliding down it. Lucky water. He grabbed my hand and pulled me up before we both ran to the little tent that held dry towels.

As soon as we were wrapped up we darted for the hotel and up to our room leaving a trail of dripping water behind us. We reached our room and dashed inside. The hotel air-conditioning left goosebumps all over my body and I'd begun to shiver violently, maybe we shouldn't have stayed out in the rain for so long.

"Shit you're freezing Sasha!" Jake cried. He pulled me to the bed and wrapped me in the spare blankets rubbing my arms up and down to create friction.

"You stay here and I'll run you a hot bath" he whispered to me before pecking my lips and walking to the bathroom. I heard the sound of rushing water and I smiled at how caring Jake seemed to be. None of my ex-boyfriends had taken so much care of me and it felt odd to be taken care of when I was usually the one doing the caring.

Jake's POV

I sat on the edge of the Jacuzzi watching the steaming hot water rise. I couldn't get my mind off Sasha. She was so beyond what I originally thought her to be. She was so prim and proper in the office, so organised and professional that I never would have thought this fiery lust filled woman prowled underneath.

I shut the taps off and walked over to the bedroom to find her lying against the pillows asleep. I chuckled and walked over to her. Her bottom lip fluttered with every breathe and I felt my cock start to harden at the thought of her lips doing something else.

"Sash... Sasha wake up honey" Her eyelids open wearily and her gaze focused on me. "Come on, let's get you in the tub"

She followed me to the bathroom and moaned when she saw the hot Jacuzzi. My cock stiffened to full alert at the sound of her moan. It was one of the most amazing sounds I'd ever heard in my life! Without warning she dropped her towel and I was instantly aware that she'd taken off her tiny bikini.

My eyes zeroed onto her full breasts and her nipples that were puckered tightly and more than ready for my teeth to pull on. She stepped into the tub and the steam swirled around her smooth legs before her whole body was dipped in the water.

"Well, are you planning on standing there or joining me stud?" she purred. She spread her arms across the edge of the tub making her chest stick out and her breasts poke forward.

My mouth watered and I quickly stripped off my towel and ridiculous trunks before almost diving into the water. I was that ready for her. She laughed at my urgency and I swam over to her trapping her body against my own.

"I love your laugh Sasha" I whispered and ducked my head to kiss her. Our passion grew and so did our kiss. My fingers trailed over to her nipples and I pinched and rolled them between my fingertips as her breathy moan filled my mouth. She removed her lips from mine to bring them to my ear.

"Put your fingers in me Jake, I want to feel your fingers in me"

Holy shit!

I lowered my hand and swirled my fingers around her clit occasionally dipping a little into her tunnel. When she arched her back and pushed her breasts to my chest I pushed two fingers into her hot pussy and pumped them until I found a good rhythm.

My pinky brushed against something hard on the tub and I grinned. I twisted my free arm to a button on the side of the Jacuzzi and pushed it.

"Holy shit!!!" Sasha cried as the jets turned fully on and I positioned her lower body over them. "Jake! Oh my God!!!"

Her hips squirmed but I held her down pumping my fingers as the jets pulsated on her throbbing bud and I felt her walls tighten around my fingers. She exploded, screaming my name as her orgasm brought her to new heights.

Suddenly she pushed me backwards and my back hit the other side of the Jacuzzi.

"Your turn stud" she moaned and straddled me taking my whole throbbing length into her tight pussy. She slowly stroked me with her body teasing the shit out of me! I grabbed handfuls of her round ass and squeezed them and I grinded her against me and pushed myself as deep as I could go before pulling out and roughly slamming into her.

Her moans were completely wanton and they echoes around the bathroom but I never slowed down. I was too hot for her and I thrust over and over and over feeling her orgasms multiply and squeeze me tighter and tighter.

Finally I let myself release the climax I was holding back and buried myself deep as I spilt my seed into her. She collapsed and breathed heavily. We both stayed silent as we caught our breath and I hugged her tight loving the feeling of her voluptuous body pressed against my own.

After we finished in the tub I jumped out to fetch some dry towels and helped her out. I dried every inch of her body and silently congratulated myself when didn't bend her over the sink and take her from behind.

"Are you okay?" I asked Sasha as we sat on the bed watching TV in our fluffy robes.

"Yeah, I just have a stiff neck and sore back. It's nothing" she replied rubbing her shoulder.

"Here, lie down" I instructed her. I stood up and grabbed a bottle of oil from the bathroom and another towel. "Take off your robe"

I handed her the towel and she swapped the robe for her towel wrapped around her body. I pushed her shoulder gently and she laid on her stomach.

"What are you going to do?" she asked.

"I'm going to give you a massage, I've been told I have magic hands"

"Jake, you really don't have to. You're not supposed to be doing anything for me" she declared.

I ignored her and pulled the towel around her body down to just cover her ass. Her arguments that I shouldn't be doing this faltered when I squirted oil on her back and began massaging her.

My fingers glided over her satin skin on her back and massaged all the knots that collected there. I soothed her aches in her arms, hands, fingers and down her perfect legs and dainty feet. As I rubbed upwards I let my hand travel under the towel and when my fingers hit the curve of her ass I began my downward journey.

"Mmm" Sasha purred.

When I slid my hand up again I couldn't help but to cup her ass in my oil covered hands and squeeze them. I loved her ass! I kneaded her ass and moved my hands to her soaking wet pussy. I grinned and played with her dripping juices spreading them around her pussy.

I spread her legs and dipped my head to slowly lick her juices. She tasted amazing and I needed to have more! I licked and sucked and savoured her and my ears were met with constant cries of passion.

I straightened and took out my stiff cock. I pumped my dick at the sight her oiled up ass and shining wet pussy and I swear

I could explode right there. She arched her back and raised herself to her knees lifting her pussy up and spreading her lips for me to see everything clearly.

"Take me" was all she said huskily and I didn't need any more permission.

I took the head of my cock and slid it from her swollen bud across her channel and to the crease of her ass. The oil I'd spread earlier made her body slick and slippery and made me even harder.

"I know what you're thinking Jake... do it. I've never tried it, but... I want to"

I was shocked that she could read my mind but was filled with excitement!

"Are you sure?" I asked cautiously.

"Do it" she moaned pushing her ass up higher.

I gave her ass a quick slap and circled her hole with a finger. My dick throbbed at the anticipation. I pushed a finger in her ass slowly and heard her gasp.

"Does it hurt?"

"A little, but in a good way"

I grinned even more and pushed another finger into her tight hole scissoring my fingers to loosen it as I pumped my cock at the same tempo. I positioned the swollen head of my dick to her ass and pushed gently. I pushed more and more, going deeper and deeper and I swear to God her ass was squeezing my cock so tight I could burst without even having to thrust!

I squeezed my cock to the hilt and I let out a breath. I stopped to give her time to adjust but I couldn't wait any longer! I pulled back and thrust into her. It felt amazing and I began thrusting harder and longer and rubbed her clit between my fingertips.

I was so close to climaxing but I needed her to orgasm first so I thrust in deep and pinched her clit. She exploded and her ass tightened so much I climaxed and it was as though the cum was being sucked straight out of me.

"Fuck!" I shouted and buckled.

Sasha was screaming my name in pleasure and I kissed her shoulder before slowly pulling my dick out. I rolled to my side pulling her and the blanket with me and cuddled her tightly. I was beyond exhausted and felt the happiest I'd ever been in my life. But it wasn't because of all the sex.

I was happy because I held the woman I loved in my arms.

12

CHAPTER 12

Every single day and night for the rest of the week we had earth shattering sex and my body had never felt better. I was even losing weight from all this pleasurable exercise. I knew that my experiment had gone off track and now we were having sex because we craved each other's body so I knew the experiment had to stop soon.

The thought of no longer being in Jake's arms or waking up to his warmth made my heart ache but I had to keep reminding myself that it was supposed to be no strings attached sex. I felt a string of pain shock me at the thought of another man touching me the way Jake had, but I pushed it aside. Jake wasn't the type of man who fell in love.

"Grhmm" I smiled and turned my head to Jake who was frowning in his sleep. His lips pouted so adorably and a little crease showed between his eyebrows. I could feel his arms reaching out for me and I eagerly wriggled into them. Today we were leaving our little island paradise and were returning back to reality.

Back to reality also meant that the experiment was finished.

I stared at every line, curve and crease of Jake's face and every hair that covered his head. I wanted to remember my time with Jake and when we return back to boss and secretary I never wanted to leave these memories behind.

I could feel Jake's erection poking against my stomach and I felt the fluttery feeling in my lower stomach as wetness pooled between my thighs. I wanted him and by the feel of his impressive length he wanted me even in his sleep.

I slowly trailed my fingertips over his naked flesh. Down his back and his hip and I could feel his cock twitch. I smirked and lowered myself until my mouth was level with his swollen member. I slowly licked the head and massaged his sacs. He moaned in his sleep but didn't wake up.

I let my tongue leave a trail of wetness down the length of him then moved back to the tip. With pursed lips I pushed his cock into my mouth slowly until I took him completely in my mouth and began to pump him with my mouth and tongue swirling around.

"Fuck Sasha! This is the best way to wake up!" Jake growled as he finally woke up. I felt his rough hands tangle in my hair and help move my head to the rhythm he wanted. I pumped his cock faster and deeper feeling it hit the back of my throat, all the while massaging his sacs in my hand.

"Get up here you fucking sexy woman" Jake grabbed my arms and pulled me up on top of him. Every inch of our body was touching and his cock throbbed between my legs. His eyes were dark with lust and he grabbed handfuls of my ass rubbing my mound against his dick.

"Ride me Sasha, I want to feel your pussy clench around my dick when you orgasm"

I smiled and planted my feet on either side of his hips and held his thighs as I lifted myself up and down on his huge cock. It felt so amazing and when I arched my back I could feel his erection rubbing right up against my sensitive nerve bundle and I couldn't handle it! The pleasure was too much. I moved forward so my knees were next his hips and rode him hard and fast like I was racing to reach my orgasm.

I climaxed hard. My body shattered and shivers wracked my body making my breasts bounce. He slowly thrust into me making my orgasm last longer and he cupped my breasts with his hot hands and fondled them, pinching my nipples that sent lightning strikes of pleasure straight to my clit.

Then without giving me any time to recover he began pounding into me! He grabbed my hips tight and held me tight as he slammed his cock into my wet pussy over and over again as he grunted and moaned my name.

I could feel myself reaching climax point again and as I screamed out his name he slammed into me deeply and climaxed along with me. I collapsed on top of him and sighed with complete happiness. Our bodies were sick with sweat and our breathing was harsh. I didn't want this to end... but I needed to keep my head on straight and once I step into my apartment back home, that was it. It was over.

"I don't want to go home" he complained and I laughed, it was as though he was reading my mind.

"Me neither, but we have to. We have work to do"

"Damn work..."

The rest of the morning was spent packing our things and tidying up the cottage, it took a lot longer than it should because it was as though we both knew what was inevitable once we got back. I stood in the doorway as Jake packed the bags into the car and gazed around me. I was going to miss this place. Maybe one day he'd let me come back here with him, as friends of course.

"Come on Sash, we've got a plane to catch" I took one last look and followed him to the car and sighed deeply as I watched the place that would leave memories burnt into my mind forever. Jake drove the car towards the air port and I was determined to have him as much as I could before we arrived at my apartment.

I unclicked my seat belt and went straight for the buttons and zipper of his jeans.

"Sasha! What the hell are you do-" Jake started to ask but immediately stopped when I began pumping his dick.

"I want every moment to count" I whispered into his ear. I bit his ear lobe and heard him hiss. His cock was now throbbing in my hand and I bent down to gently drag my teeth over the head.

Jake's POV

I swear she wanted us to die in this car!

I was trying to concentrate on keeping the car straight as Sasha began to take my dick deep into her wet mouth. She moaned and the vibrations made me want to come straight down her throat, I don't know how I'm not at the moment.

"Oh God Sasha! You're mouth feel so good!" I groaned. She deep throated my cock and kept pumping it deeply. I growled loudly and did the worst thing I could do.

I looked down at her.

I could see my cock wet from her mouth as it dipped in and out of view from her luscious lips and I snapped my head up just in time to turn the steering wheel and keep the car from running off the road. I thrust my hips up in time with her mouth and I was so close!

"Come here" I growled.

"What?" she asked as she sat up on her knees.

I grabbed her around the waist and pulled her onto my lap as I continued to drive. I was so glad she wore a sun dress because I pulled her thong to the side and thrust my cock into her dripping wet pussy.

"Jake! We might crash!" she squealed as her delicate hands held onto my shoulders.

"It wouldn't be any different than if you continued giving me head, trust me Sasha" I groaned as I clenched the steering wheel and tried, extremely hard, to concentrate on the road as I thrust into her over and over again.

"Oh God Jake!" she cried as she took over and began grinding her sweet ass against me. I tried to hold back until she came and growled loudly when her walls clenched around my swollen dick. We climaxed at the same time and it took everything I had to not close my eyes in ecstasy.

"Damn Sasha!" I puffed out. We drove the rest of the way with her in the same position and me nibbling on her perky breasts. By the time we got to the airport I practically shoved her in the back seat and drove into her again! Her legs were curled around my waist and with every thrust her feet hit the roof of the car.

"Yes! Oh my God!" she was crying over and over.

She'd already orgasmed twice and was climaxing for the third time when I let myself go and spilt my seed, spurting it in her throbbing pussy.

"I feel like a teenager again" I breathed heavily. There was something about Sasha that made me feel more energetic and younger. I was so close to telling her I loved her but I didn't know if she felt the same. I knew she was finishing the 'experiment' when we get back to reality and that would leave me as just her boss.

"Are you up for another round at being in the mile high club Mr Stone" she purred as she ran a thumb down my temple. Her voice and the way she looked at made me think that maybe she does love me too, but then my clenched when she called me Mr Stone. It was like a stab of reality, even though she used it to be seductive.

Sasha's POV

The flight was amazing. Well, the flight itself was normal but the sex on the plane was amazing.

I closed my eyes and smiled. We had sex twice during the flight and while the plane was descending Jake decided he wanted to taste every inch between my legs. The fluttery feeling from the landing and the climax that made me explode was more than I could handle.

I blushed when I remembered the captain wondering if the flight scared me because he could hear me screaming.

Now we were in a cab on the way to my apartment and it just seemed against my luck that every single light was green. I wanted another quickie, another touch, another kiss. One last 'something' that included Jake touching me but no, it wouldn't be long enough.

"So uh, Jake..." I cleared my throat when y voice seemed hoarse, "now that we've left the island everything between us-"

"Will go back to normal, I know" he interrupted me. I looked over at him and saw that his face was blank. It was strange. Ever since I asked him if he would help me with my experiment I'd been able to read him like a book but now there was nothing there to read. He was blank, completely closed off.

And it hurt.

The cab stopped outside my apartment and Jake helped me with my luggage. He dropped them inside my door and stood rigidly at the entrance.

"So, I'll see you bright and early at work Sasha"

"Yeah... see you Monday Jake" I replied. He nodded once and turned to leave and I shut the door quickly so I didn't have to see him walk away.

I needed a hot bubble bath, I decided. That should help, along with a large tub of ice cream. I ran a hot bath and added more bubbles than necessary. I stripped out of my clothes and slowly stepped into the hot water sighing as the heat relaxed my tense muscles.

I grabbed my body soap and rubbed it across my skin but as each stroke went memories of Jake's touch lingered in my mind. So my hands travelled down to my nipples and I imagined Jake's teeth pulling on them gently. I moaned and urged my hands to slip lower, I circled my clit and teasingly dipped my fingertip into my channel.

"Jake..." I whispered huskily into the steamy air and I imagined him being the one whose fingers were causing me pleasure. My fingers dipped inside and I added another I was pumping myself and imagining it was now Jake's huge cock sliding in and out of me. I tipped my head back and felt it thud against the edge of the tub.

His name passed through my lips again and soon I could feel my walls tightening and clenching, almost pulling at my fingers and when my climax hit I cried out Jake's name. After several seconds I opened my eyes and felt the sadness hit me again when I realised that Jake was, in fact, not there and it was all my imagination.

I knew why I was so bothered but I never expected it to happen. Not with Jake, this was supposed to be a no-strings attached experiment. But I guess it's something no one can control.

I was in love with Jake.

13

⸻ ◆ ⸻

CHAPTER 13

His hot breath warmed the delicate skin of my neck and he lightly nipped and kissed my collarbone. The room was humid and beads of sweat rolled from our naked bodies. I sighed in ecstasy as Jakes big, rough hands slid up the sides of my hips and grasped them tightly and rolled his tongue down my over sensitive nipples. He paid so much attention to my already erect nipples and I felt my body tense and explode at the simple touch.

"Fuck me Jake. Please!" I moaned as I clawed the smooth skin of his back and he grabbed his swollen cock and rubbed the head around and around my clit building the tension I had inside of me and when he slid his length into my core my legs shot up and wrapped around his lean waist.

My fingernails were digging into his shoulders and with every deep thrust I slid further up the bed until I had to hold my hands against the wall. He slammed into me harder and deeper and faster and my climaxes rolled together to create a one long explosion and the feeling was so intense tears sprung into my eyes and I smiled as Jake threw his head back to roar as he found his climax and thrust so deeply inside me I'm surprised he didn't get lost in me.

"Sasha... I lo-"

My alarm clock beeped loudly, shouting at me to get out of bed and get ready for work. No! No, no, no!

"Argh!" I screamed as I grabbed my pillow and slammed it hard against the clock until it fell from the night stand and broke. "Stupid alarm clock" I grumbled.

I flopped back into my warm bed and sighed deeply. Today everything went back to how it was before I saw the real Jake Stone. He was Mr Stone and I was Miss Montgomery. Life sucked right now.

I rolled myself out of bed and dragged my feet to the shower making sure it was a cold one. My dream was intense and I could feel the remnants of my climaxes wash away with the cold water. I stepped out and changed into a black high waisted pencil skirt with white silk top under a fitted black blazer. Nothing says 'back to work and stop fucking the boss' like business attire.

I pulled my hair up into a tight bun and slid my black pumps on before grabbing my bag and heading out to the nearest Starbucks for my and Jake's coffees. After picking up our coffees I made my way to work and as the ding of the elevator told me I was on my floor I put on a nonchalant face and walked to my office.

Everything seemed the same. Everything looked the same. But the fact that there wouldn't be any secret flings in the office or on the desks made the day seem like it would last forever. I placed Jake's coffee on his desk and went back to my office to check through the emails and letters.

"Good morning Sasha" I jumped at the sound of Jake's silky voice and quickly pulled myself together.

"Good morning Jake, you have emails to go through this morning and a Mr Smithson to call back, he says it's urgent. I doubt it is, but I'm just passing on the message-..."

"Slow down there Sasha. It's only eight o'clock" he chuckled. Damn I missed his carefree chuckles in the mornings. Pull yourself together!

"Sorry sir"

"Sir?" he asked raising an eyebrow.

"Jake..." I blushed. He was staring at me with dark eyes and I could feel my stomach flutter so I pulled my eyes away and cleared my throat. "I'll be in my office if you need anything"

Before I could do anything stupid, like jump over his desk and rip his clothes off, I quickly turned on my heel and escaped to my office leaving the door half closed.

Jake's POV

Today was going to be torture!

How the hell was I supposed to concentrate on work when she was on the other side of the wall in those drool worthy tight clothes that hugged every delicious curve of her body. I read the same sentence on the email I was reading for the tenth time and gave up. I wasn't going to get anywhere.

I pushed my chair back and stretched backwards slyly looking through the gap in the door to peek at Sasha. She'd taken off her blazer and her silk top showed the curve of her generous breasts and she was currently stretching back like I was.

Her top two buttons popped open at the movement and just the sight of her cleavage made me drool. She turned her head and her eyes caught mine. I jumped in surprise and the wheels of my chair jerked forward quickly effectively sending me falling over backwards.

"Oh my God! Jake are you okay?" I heard Sasha cry.

Nope, I think I might just kill myself right now thank you. I stayed on the ground and acted as though I was meant to fall flat on my flat.

"I'm fine Sasha. I'm just tired" I said lamely.

She took hold of my arm and helped me up while I dusted off non-existent dirt from my trousers; suffice to say it was a bit awkward. I glanced over to the clock and noticed that it was past lunch.

"I think I might have vacation mind" I said chuckling lightly and ran a hand through my hair, "I can't concentrate properly on work. How about we finish up early and start new tomorrow?" I suggested.

Her face lit up with a bright smile and nodded eagerly. I watched her walk to her office and switch her computer off while tidying up her desk. I did the same and just when she came back in to say her goodbyes I interrupted her.

"Did you want to go for lunch Sasha?" I asked. I'd missed her touches, kisses and moans last night and had to relieve myself more than once whenever her face popped into my mind.

"Oh uh... I'm not sure Jake" she replied. It looked like she was stuck between decisions and I just wanted another few hours with her.

"Just friends. Or even boss and secretary" I added holding my hands up in innocence. She thought about it for a few seconds then slowly nodded with a little smile pulling at the corner of her mouth.

"Just friends" she said quietly.

Sasha's POV

I think I'm about two seconds away from exploding!

We headed out to a quiet restaurant and sat in a corner booth. The entire time between leaving the office and now Jake had found every opportunity to touch me. The soft touch of his warm hand on my lower back as he guided me through a crowd, a bump of a shoulder or a brush of a leg... it was like torture!

I was beginning to think that doing my experiment on my boss was a horrible idea, but immediately brushed the thought away. The time I spent with Jake was by far the best time I'd ever had in my life and I'd never take it back.

We were talking and laughing and before we knew it, it was already dark outside. "Oh wow, I should get home. I have a few things to go through with the paperwork from the office" I sighed.

He sighed deeply and I must've been kidding myself when I thought I saw a sadness flash through his eyes. "Come on, I'll drop you off"

We caught a cab together and for some reason Jake thought it was necessary to walk me all the way up to my apartment. The sexual tension between us was so thick you could bounce on it like a jumping castle.

We stepped out from the elevator and I breathed in the fresh air. His cologne was driving me insane and I just wanted to rip his clothes off. I tried to kill some time as I dug through my purse for my keys and when I found them I felt his large hand swallow mine.

"Having a little trouble with the keys Miss Montgomery?" he whispered huskily.

"Uh... no, I'm just a little cold and my hands are shaking..."

He stepped forward and pressed his front to my back and I could feel his obvious erection poking into the curve of my ass. "Let me help you then"

He moved our hands to the door and unlocked it. He swung the door open and together we walked inside before he kicked it shut and spun me around against the wooden door. Our fronts were pressed together and I was getting frustrated with our clothing being the way.

He trailed his nose up the side of my neck and when his mouth reached my ear he whispered " I haven't been able to get you out of my mind Sasha" I shivered as his breath tickled my skin. "Have you missed me as much as I missed you?"

"Yes" I replied but my throat wasn't working and I doubt he was able to hear it so I nodded to confirm again.

"You kept flashing through my mind last night" he took my hand and placed it against his stiff member, "The memories of you made me so hard and instead of your warm body I had to be the one to relieve myself. Did you touch yourself Sasha?" He was whispering as his hand trailed up my thigh and teased the vee of my legs.

"Did you pretend that your hands pinching your nipples were my teeth? And your fingers caressing your pussy was my cock?" He pressed his chest against my breasts and his hands were slowly pulling my skirt up until it bunched around my hips.

"Yes!" I croaked. Oh God he was making me so wet, my body was dying to have him inside and yet I was helpless to move from where I was.

"Say you want me Sasha. Say you want me to fuck you every way possible until we collapse from exhaustion"

"Yes! Jake, God please! Fuck me! Fuck me now! NOW!" I basically screamed as I sagged against the door.

Before I knew it his panties were gone, his pants were done and my legs were being wrapped around his hips. He pushed into my throbbing core and I cried out arching my back. He filled me so completely and deeply that I moaned and panted as he brought us to the peak of our pleasure. I was barely coming back down from cloud nine when he kicked his pants off and walked us over to the kitchen bench and flipped me over so my ass stuck out.

"You know Sasha, you were the only one I'd ever tried anal with before and I'm afraid you've had me hooked on the feeling of your tightness." He groaned as he rubbed my dripping juices all around my ass and pushed two fingers into my back hole. I cried out in pleasure and pain but he bent down and while he scissored his fingers in my ass he licked my pussy and teased my clit.

I was screaming in ecstasy and just before I could climax he stood up and slowly thrust in my ass. He groaned loudly and squeezed my hips tightly as he slowly pushed in and pulled out increasing his tempo. His hands ripped open my silk blouse and pulled the cups of my bra down letting my breasts spill out. He cupped them and rolled my nipples between his fingers as he slammed into my ass over and over again.

My climax hit me quickly and he cried out as well as my body squeezed him tightly. "Shit Sasha!" he growled in pleasure.

We were panting and I flinched when he carefully pulled his cock from me. "I can't get enough of you Sasha" he gasped.

I wanted to tell him I felt the same, that I wanted to spend forever in his arms but Jacob Stone was not a man who married and settled down. I was looking for marriage and kids and even though the chemistry between us were explosive I knew he wouldn't want to marry me. I needed him tonight and if tonight was all I was going to get then I would tire the poor man out before heading back to our normal lives.

If I couldn't handle it... then I'd have no choice but to quit my job.

"Stay the night Jake... let me make you feel good" I said.

His eyes darkened with lust again and he scooped me up bridal style and headed towards my bedroom. He laid me on the bed and stripped me of all my clothing so I lay naked on my bed sheets staring at his amazing naked body.

"So beautiful" he said and kissed my lips tenderly. We kissed for what seemed like hours while his hands memorised every inch of my skin and soon his lips followed. He was licking my pussy like tonight was his last night alive and after I orgasmed I flipped him roughly onto his back.

"I'm not letting you have all the fun big guy" I said eyeing his huge cock that stood tall and proud. I leaned down and took him in my mouth completely until he hit the back of my throat. I deep throated him until tears sprung into my eyes and massage his sacs. I continued to pleasure him and I could tell he was close to coming. He tangled his hands into my hair and pulled me up letting me straddle his rock hard length.

I slowly slid myself onto him and groaned at how he seemed to feel amazing in me every single fucking time!

He grabbed my hips and lifted me up and impaled me back down and soon I was bouncing on him like a cowgirl riding a bull, my walls gripped and tightened around his cock and I tried to hold back to make the pleasure last longer but his dick was so hard and thick and grinding against my g-spot that it was impossible to hold back.

I screamed his name as I came and grinded my hips hard against his as he shouted my name as well. I felt like jello and collapsed against his sculpted chest. The words 'I love you' nearly slipped from my mouth but I managed to hold it back and not ruin the beautiful moment we'd shared.

We spent the rest of the night and early morning having sex all around the apartment. In the shower, on the bed again, on the floor, the couch, on the balcony and against every single wall. We collapsed on my bed in exhaustion and fell asleep wrapped in each other's arms.

I couldn't do this... I couldn't work for him and pretend that I wasn't totally and completely head over heels in love with the man. Tomorrow morning I was handing in my two weeks' notice and leaving the job and man I loved.

"What do you mean you're quitting?!" Jake shouted in confusion and anger.

I stood awkwardly in front of his desk with my arms crossing each other as he stared wide eyed at me holding my two weeks' notice in front of him.

"I was offered a good job at another company Jake, quite a while ago and they're just waiting on me" It was the truth. I'd received a call from another shipping company a few months ago and they were so desperate to have me that they were willing to wait for me to say yes. At first I said no, but they told me to keep their number and call them if I ever changed my mind.

"What are they offering to pay you?" he growled angrily as he stood up, "I'll double whatever they're willing to pay and give you even better benefits!"

I sighed. This wasn't going as good as I thought it would. "It's not the money Jake. It's a company overseas. They're situated in Australia"

His back went rigid and he snapped his head towards me, "So that's it, is it? We get to know each other, have mind blowing sex and then you up and leave?"

I stuttered as I tried to come up with an answer. "Jake it's not like that... I-"

"No. I get it... Fine. Set up interviews for your replacement and have one picked in a week's time" his voice was void of all emotion and he sat back down in his chair and tapped away at the keyboard as if he just dismissed me and I was no longer in the room.

I lifted my chin and walked to my office closing the door that connected our offices.

Jake's POV

She was leaving me.

The woman I fell in love with is leaving me and made it plain obvious that she didn't love me. I felt like such an idiot. Of course she didn't love me! She offered me no strings attached sex for an experiment and that's what I agreed to. She didn't ask for marriage, or a relationship or a future.

I slammed my fist into the keyboard making a few keys break off. My dick was still sore from the night of sex we shared and yet it felt like my heart had been blown to pieces then trampled on by overweight elephants.

"Give it up Jake... she doesn't want you..." I said to myself and stood at the window watching the crowds of people below going about their day.

Sasha's POV

A week had passed and I was beyond frustrated with the women who had applied for my job. At first I assessed them and cut the list down considerably separating the idiots from the potential good secretaries. Then I noticed I became more critical. I started crossing off the women who were tall and lean, women who were too beautiful or too smart and I was making finding a replacement extremely difficult.

Jake and I had barely spoken to each other besides what needed to be said for work and I hated the distance that was between us. I called the Australian shipping company and let them know that I was willing to work for them and they were only too happy to hear the news. My ticket was paid for and I'd packed the things I wanted to bring with me overseas.

It was hard to be in my apartment though. Every single thing reminded me of Jake and our night of passion together only a week ago and I couldn't stop the tears that threatened to spill everytime I thought of him.

This was for the best, I told myself. Better to do this now than do something stupid like confess my love for him and get rejected by him. I was losing weight from the stress of finding a replacement in time and my feelings for Jake and the thought of food had no appeal to me.

The deadline was drawing closer and I finally was able to pick between two women for the job. I went for the less appealing woman, though I don't know why. The prettier woman was easily the best for the job and yet I couldn't find it in me to hire her. What if Jake found her pretty and decided to make her his next bed buddy.

I shook my head. No, he never usually mixed business with pleasure. 'But he did with you' a voice in my head whispered. I let out an aggravated sigh, I was different! I told myself. But it shouldn't matter anyway because I'm leaving!

"I guess this is goodbye then" Jake said emotionlessly as I finished my last day. His usual bright eyes were dull and it looked like he hadn't been sleeping properly lately. His hair was dishevelled and he held a light stubble across his strong jaw.

"Yes, I guess so…" I stuck my hand out to shake his hand but he just stared at it like it was an alien. Embarrassed, I let my hand drop but squeaked when he quickly wrapped his sturdy arms around me and hugged me tight. I felt like I was in heaven once again and I wrapped my arms around his waist breathing in his scent.

"I'll miss you Sash" he mumbled and I had to use everything in me to not cry.

"I'll miss you too Jake" I whispered back.

He let go too quickly and I suddenly felt alone. The loneliness and sadness I felt was so strong I had the urge to throw up but brushed away the feelings.

"I'll be back to visit soon and make sure you haven't run the company to the ground" I joked lightly. He smiled and his whole face lit up. He hadn't been smiling much lately and I smiled that the last time I saw Jake would be him smiling at me.

"Goodbye Jake" I said and quickly turned to leave.

Two months later

"Are you sure you're okay Sasha?" Caleb, my new boss, asked me with concern. I had my head on my desk and was currently trying to fight off another wave of nausea.

"I'm fine. I guess I'm still not used to the Australian humidity" I replied. The humidity and weather changes in Australia were so crazy that it quickly made me sick and I thought that I'd be over it by now.

"Why don't you take the rest of the day off and see a doctor?" he suggested. "We're not busy today anyway"

"Thanks, I think I will" He patted me on the shoulder and I quickly packed my things up and grabbed my purse.

As I waited for the doctor to see me I watched all the other sick people in the waiting room. Old couples looking through cross words in the magazines, children playing with the toys and books in the corner while other adults eyed the children as though they'd make them sicker with every cough or sneeze.

"Sasha Montgomery?"

I stood up and followed the doctor to the room as sat as she shut the door. "So... what can I do for you today?"

I explained to her how I thought the humidity was causing my waves of nausea and other symptoms I'd been having since coming to Australia and she sat and nodded while I spoke.

"Would you mind if I had a urine sample?" she asked. I nodded and walked to the bathroom, returning with the sample in a plastic jar.

"Thank you" she said. She stood up and rummaged through some drawers before taking out a paper strip and dipping it into the sample. After checking it and disposing of the sample she sat back down and smiled at me.

"Well Sasha, the reason why you've been feeling ill lately is because you're pregnant. Congratulations!"

I stared at her, not quite registering what she was saying, "I'm sorry what?"

"You're pregnant. When was the last time you had your period?"

I calculated the weeks and realised it'd been over two and a half months since my last period. I hadn't even noticed seeing as I was stressed a lot nowadays. "About two and a half months" I told her. I was in shock and silently thanked God that I stopped taking the pill months ago so it didn't affect the baby growing in me. "But, I was on the pill... how could I...?"

"The pill is not 100% effective. The only way to avoid pregnancies is to refrain from having sex" she answered for me.

I left the doctor a little while later with brochures for pregnancies and still in a state of shock. I was pregnant. I was pregnant with Jake's baby.

14

CHAPTER 14

A fortnight had passed since I found out about my pregnancy and I was beginning to wish I hadn't. It seemed as though ever since I found out, my body made sure to catch up with all the morning sickness I'd missed and I was currently lying in bed wishing I could just die. I told my boss the next day and he sent me home saying that I had overworked myself and needed to rest for the sake of my health and the baby.

I only dragged myself out of bed to throw up in the bathroom or grab something to eat. I had a huge appetite now and the weight I'd lost months ago had come back three fold. Apparently I was twenty-two weeks pregnant and due to have another ultrasound where I could find out the gender of the baby. My baby bump began to make an appearance last week and grew quickly so that unless I was wearing an extra baggy shirt, it was obvious I was pregnant.

Having an abortion was never an option. As soon as the initial shock passed I fell completely in love with this baby and knew it would be my number one priority. As for her daddy... I hadn't had the guts to pick up the phone and call him. What would I say?

'Oh hey there Jake, remember how I offered you no strings attached sex? Well, apparently there was one string attached and it's in the form of an umbilical cord attached to the baby we made currently growing in my womb. How's business been?'

No... obviously not.

As I contemplated how long it would take to crawl to the bathroom a knock sounded at my door. Ugh, who the hell would be visiting me? I hadn't made any close friends and the only person who knocked on my door was the fedex man who brought my boxes up to my apartment.

The knocking got louder and more impatient yet no one yelled or asked if I was home. I considered letting them continue but after five minutes of constant knocking I groaned and flipped the dirty sheets off of me to drag myself to the door. Whoever the hell was knocking the crap out of my door would be in for a gruesome surprise when they saw me.

I glanced at my reflection in the TV screen as I passed it to the door and grimaced when I saw my tangled hair and dull skin. I hadn't showered yet and my baggy clothes were all wrinkled. The knocking continued and I rolled my eyes.

"I'm coming damnit!" I shouted.

I unlocked the door and threw it open.

"Surprise!!! How have you-... Sasha! What the hell happened to you? Are you okay?" The incessant knocker was my best friend Jenna and I had to say that I was utterly surprised that she was here. I hadn't seen her since the day I left for Australia and she had gone as far as begging me on her knees not to leave.

"Uh... I'm fine" I finally answered. "Come on in Jenna, how've you been?"

She eyed me sceptically before walking in dragging her luggage behind her and sat herself on the sofa.

"I've been good... Jake's been a pain in the ass lately though, just in case you were wondering" I rolled my eyes at her and shook my head.

"Well that's good for you and too bad for him. Now, may I ask what this random visit is about, not that I don't appreciate it"

"Nothing" she said a little too quickly, "Can't a girl travel across the world without notice to visit her best friend?"

"Apparently not..." I said but quickly stopped when I felt a wave of nausea hit me. I covered my mouth and ran to the bathroom as fast as I could without making it worse. I burst through the door and heaved up my stomach contents before cleaning myself off. I turned to leave and came face to face with Jenna.

"What's wrong with you?" she asked sincerely.

I sighed deeply and walked over to the sofa, gesturing for her to follow me. After she plopped herself next to me I lost all the words I'd planned to say. My mind came up blank and I opened and closed my mouth like a fish.

"Well...?"

It was too hard to say the words, so I simply stood up in front of her and slowly lifted my baggy t-shirt to reveal my baby bump while I gently caressed the hidden baby within me. Several expressions crossed her face: confusion, realisation, shock then happiness and wonder.

"You're pregnant?" she whispered staring at my swollen belly. I nodded and her face lit up like the sun before she screamed in joy. "I HAVE A NEPHEW OR NIECE!"

She began laughing and hugged me tightly before holding me back at arm's length, "This is my nephew or niece in here right?"

"Of COURSE it's your niece or nephew!" I retorted slapping her arm.

"Oh my God! Oh my God! Does Jake know?!" she squealed.

I pulled a face and slowly shook my head. "No, not yet. .. Don't worry I wasn't going to keep it from him but I just couldn't think of a way to tell him. Jenna I offered him no strings attached sex and here I am carrying his baby!"

I broke down in tears.

This baby was causing me to have crazy mood swings and one moment I was smiling at the TV show I was watching then crying for no apparent reason. It was horrifying! Jenna wrapped me in a tight hug and just held me while I cried.

"You're coming back home with me Sasha. I don't care what you think or say. You don't have anyone here and you've always been family to me but now it's technically true!" Jenna argued with her.

"I barely started my job a few months ago Jenna, what would they think about me?"

"Who the hell cares?! You obviously can't work the way you're feeling now anyway and they'd understand for sure"

I thought about it and knew she was right. I had more than enough savings thanks to my generous pay from Jake to go without working for a few months and this was something I really needed to tell Jake in person, not over the phone.

"Okay"

The next day was my ultrasound and Jenna was nearly as excited as I was. She was bouncing on the spot speedily talking about buying clothes and baby things once the gender was found out. My bladder was bursting and I couldn't wait to get the ultrasound over with so I go to the bathroom.

I was called in and Jenna followed with a massive smile on her face.

"Now lay back on here and we'll get started, Sasha" the lady instructed. I hopped onto the cushion bed and lifted my blouse to show my swelling belly. I winced as the lady squirted cold gel on and she offered me a smile. It felt funny when she rubbed around looking at the ultrasound and taking measurements then finally after a few minutes she stilled her hand and pressed a button.

A thumping sound filled the room. "Hear that? That's your baby's heartbeat, it's nice and strong as well so that's very good!" Tears sprung into my eyes as I listened to the little thump-thump-thump of my unborn baby. I looked over to Jenna and she was already openly crying. "Now, did you want to know the sex of the baby?"

"Yes!" Jenna and I said in unison and we waited patiently as the lady prodded around.

"Now... see these three lines here?" she asked as she pointed to three slightly bolder lines on the screen. We nodded. "That shows that us that you are having a little girl"

I blinked. A girl. I'm having a little baby girl!

"Wow" was all I could utter. I was speechless as images of a little girl who looked exactly like her daddy ran through my head. She was going to be beautiful, absolutely beautiful.

Jenna began to bawl her eyes out and the words 'girl', 'princess' and 'shopping' were all I was able to comprehend. We finished up inside and I was given a cd with images of the scan along with a video of my little baby girl squirming around and an audio of her heartbeat.

"Sasha! I'm going to have a niece!" Jenna squealed when we stepped outside the building. We screamed together with huge smiles permanently etched onto our faces as we squeezed each other in a tight embrace.

"Come on Jenna, I have a lot of packing to do"

The next few days were rushed. My boss wasn't surprised to hear that I was quitting and moving back with Jenna. He let me go with a bonus as a baby shower present and I didn't even need to give him two week's notice.

In no time Jenna and I were on the plane back home and while I was excited and calm before, now I was a nervous wreck. It was time to tell Jake.

"Okay... so I'll leave you to get settled back for a few days. If you need anything at all, no matter the time of day or night you call me alright?" Jenna assured me. I kept nodding as she spoke. "And Sasha... you need to tell him, soon"

"I know... I will. Just-just give me time okay?" She gave me a pointed look.

"Your time is limited sweety" Then with one last hug she left.

This was one of the reasons why I loved Jenna. She was always there to have my back and yet she pointed me in the right direction when I got a little lost. I plopped onto the sofa with my pregnancy magazine and flipped through pages when I came across an article about baby names.

I smiled. I couldn't believe I was having a baby girl! I looked through the names listed and rejected each one. I wanted something different and beautiful. I pulled a face at the too common names and raised an eyebrow at the odd names I found, but then the perfect name hit me.

Annalise.

It was beautiful and perfect for my little baby girl.

"I can't wait to meet you Annalise" I cooed as I rubbed my stomach. I jumped when she kicked my hand and stared in shock at the spot that moved. Quick as a flash I grabbed my cell phone and dialled Jenna's number.

"Hell-"

"JENNA! SHE KICKED! SHE KICKED! SHE KICKED! GET OVER HERE NOW!" I screamed in excitement at the phone.

"The phone was filled was filled with car horns and a squealing Jenna and in five minutes she was back at my door.

"LET ME TOUCH YOUR STOMACH WOMAN!" she yelled as she leapt for my protruding belly. I laughed as Annalise kicked and squirmed against her hands and Jenna was positively beaming with happiness.

"She loves me!"

"Of course she does!"

His hot rough hands dragged themselves over my ass and I pried my eyes open to stare into his eyes. They were large and dark with lust as he squeezed me tightly and pulled me hard against his throbbing erection. His breath caressed my cheekbones and he kissed the corner of my mouth.

"Jake" I whispered. He cut off any more words by holding a finger to my lips.

"Shh... I need you Sasha" he declared before swooping down and capturing my lips with a hot and heavy kiss.

I held his shoulders and pushed, rolling him to his back. But as I was about to land on his sculpted chest I felt myself falling further and further, what the hell? Jake disappeared and I felt myself free falling into darkness. I screamed and woke up suddenly when I fell off the bed onto the ground.

Pain ripped through me when I hit the carpeted floor and I cried as I felt fluid between my legs. No! Not my baby! I wiped my fingers across my thighs and saw what I dreaded most. Blood.

Jake's POV

I slammed my empty glass against the bar after finishing off another shot of whisky. She was here. She was back in the same country and I didn't even have the guts to call her or 'drop by'. Jenna had been on a high having her best friend back and it was getting on my nerves a little.

I didn't know why I was having these jealous feelings about Jenna seeing her and not me. I could always just... call her and ask how the new job was going? My fuzzy brain thought up the different excuses and ideas of what I could say to Sasha and before I knew it my hand was already dialling her number.

The phone rang and rang and rang before it went to her voicemail. I continued to call, not caring that it was already late and became more frustrated with each unanswered call.

"Fuck this! I'll just go visit her!" I dropped several bills for the bartender and nearly fell off my stool when I slid off.

I was a little more than tipsy but not enough to have my motor skills challenged, so I hopped into my car and drove off to Sasha's apartment. Every minute that passed I became more eager to see her beautiful face. I'm sure she wouldn't be too angry to see me at... I looked at my watch and frowned when it read two-thirty in the morning.

By the time I reached her apartment I'd sobered up and wondering if this was really a good idea. Hell, I was already here I might as well just see if she was alright, she wasn't answering her phone after all.

I trudged up the stairs and stopped outside her door. Damn, the memories of holding her naked against the inside of that door came flooding back and I was suddenly fighting back a monster erection. Stop it Jake! That part of your life with her is over. She made that more than clear!

I knocked on the door and waited.

Nothing.

I knocked again a little harder, which was again answered by nothing. I sighed and turned to leave when a high pitched sound caught my ears. I listened intently and heard it again.

"Sasha!?" I cried at the door. "Open the door Sasha!"

Her screams of pain became louder and louder and I didn't wait a second longer. I took a step back and launched my foot at her door ripping the lock off and splintering the wood. "Sasha! Where are you!"

"Jake! Please help me!" She cried from her bedroom. I ran over to her and was shocked to see Sasha on the ground with blood seeping through her shorts. Her face was contorted in agony and her hand gripped at her stomach through her baggy shirt.

"I'm taking you to the hospital" I said immediately. I wasn't wasting time calling an ambulance, I bent down and scooped her up bridal style and hurried out the door to my car before speeding away.

15

—— ◆ ——

CHAPTER 15

Jake's POV

I paced the hallway of the hospital waiting for a damn doctor to stop in front of me and tell me what the hell is going on with Sasha. I ran a shaking hand through my already tousled hair and heaved a sigh. This wasn't helping.

I walked over to the elevator and hit the up button. As I waited, a tall voluptuous red head came to stand by me. Everything about her screamed fake and I suppose could be any plastic surgeons' miracle. Her hair was bright red, obviously not natural, her face was flawlessly painted with make up and her body curved in all the right places... also not natural.

I crossed my arms over my chest and wondered why the hell the elevator was taking so long, then mumbled 'finally' when the doors dinged open. Being a gentleman I let her walk through first and hit the floor where the canteen was before asking her floor.

"Oh... same as you" she smiled brightly.

I grunted in response and stared at the metals doors. The doors chimed at every floor and more people flooded in. I squashed myself into the corner and with every new person the red head shuffled closer to me until our shoulders touched.

Finally we hit the ground floor and I pushed past people not caring if I was being rude, I was too wound up to care. I stuck my hands into my pockets and walked straight to the cafe for a strong coffee. This was exactly what I needed. I sat down at a small metal table and sipped at my coffee letting my mind wonder what the hell happened to Sasha and why she was bleeding so much.

A loud scraping next to me shook me out of my thoughts and I saw that the red head had pulled out the chair next to me.

"Mind if I sit here handsome?" she smiled holding her own coffee. I obviously glanced around us and saw about ten empty tables then looked at her wondering if she was being serious.

"Go ahead" I replied. She grinned and sat down on the chair crossing a leg over the other making her skirt creep up her thigh. As soon as she settled into her chair and leaned forward to make conversation I stood up roughly and walked away. I seriously wasn't in the mood for women like her. I drank my coffee as I made my way back to the emergency entrance and took out my cell phone to call Jenna.

"Hello?" she answered groggily. I winced when I realised that it was three-thirty in he morning and she was obviously sleeping.

"Jen… I have bad news"

"Bad news…?" she asked slowly. "What do you mean?"

"It's Sasha… She…" I sighed, "Jen, Sasha's-"

"Oh my God…! She told you didn't she?" I frowned. She told me? What the hell did that mean?

"Told me what?" I asked curiously.

"Uh… that she… quit her job… in Australia" she replied hesitantly. I furrowed my brows at her tone. Jenna was never that good at lying and I knew she was hiding something from me, but for the moment I let it slide.

"Uh…no. I went over to Sasha's apartment and found her bleeding on the floor so now I'm going out of my mind here in the hospital waiting for a damn doctor to tell me what the hell happened and how she is!!!" I cried into the phone getting louder with every word.

"Shit! I'm on my way right now!" She yelled back. I heard the door slam and the line went dead.

Jenna was running to my side within fifteen minutes, "Has the doctor been here yet?!"

I shook my head. "No, not yet" I held her elbow and sat her down on the uncomfortable plastic chairs making sure she faced me. "You know something. There's no point in denying it because you suck at lying. Now what aren't you telling me?"

I thought that maybe the stress of not knowing what was happening with Sasha was literally making me go insane. Maybe I was overreacting to a little stumble of words on the phone, but when I noticed Jenna's eyes looking more than a little guilty I thought that maybe I was onto something.

"Jenna..." I growled warningly.

"If Sasha hasn't told you yet then it's not my place to tell you Jake" she winced. I was about to demand she tell me when a doctor walked over to us. Immediately my thoughts about Jenna's secret was forgotten as I waited for the news.

"What happened doc? Is Sasha okay?" I asked as soon as he was within earshot.

"Sasha is fine. Her pain subsided but she was dehydrated and hadn't been eating well so we're going to keep her overnight just to make sure she's okay" he paused and his business face disappeared and was replaced with sorrow. "However, I'm sorry to say that she lost the baby"

What.

The.

Fuck.

My mind froze and I stared at the doctor thinking he might have the wrong Sasha. Sasha's... pregnant? No. I corrected myself. She was pregnant. She lost the baby. Oh my God. I turned to Jenna, ignoring the doctor, and she looked absolutely heart-broken.

"You knew" I blamed her. The doctor cleared his throat and announced that Sasha was in room 512 but couldn't have visitors until eight o'clock before turning away. "You knew Jenna. You knew she was pregnant"

Jenna's brown eyes widened and tears were streaking down her tired face. "Yes" she choked out.

"How long?" I was quite surprised at how calm my voice sounded.

"Since I visited Sasha in Australia. Jake, you need to understand that it wasn't my place to tell you. I told Sasha to tell you and she was, she really was going to, but she didn't know how to do it"

"How far along was she?" I whispered. I couldn't speak loud anymore, the pain of knowing that Sasha had to go through all this alone struck me straight at my heart.

"She was about twenty-two weeks"

I staggered backwards and fell into the chair behind me. There was no doubt that the baby was mine. Besides I didn't believe that Sasha was one to jump back into the sack with another guy after what we had... right?

I growled loudly in frustration. "My baby. She was pregnant with my baby!" I stood up from the chair and kicked at the plastic making it crack. "I need some air"

Without a second glance at my twin sister I turned and walked away taking the stairs instead of waiting for the elevator.

Sasha's POV

I stared at the IV drip that was stuck into my hand and had the urge to rip it out. Why the hell should I be taken care of when I couldn't even take care my own baby that was inside me?

I closed my eyes and felt the hot tears follow the still wet tracks of previous tears. I remembered when Jake brought me into emergency and the nurse immediately sent me in to be seen, leaving Jake outside. The doctor looked almost exactly like Dr Chase from the sitcom House and he quickly went ahead asking questions about the pregnancy. He took blood samples and even took an ultrasound and did the whole speculum thing.

When he told me that I'd miscarried I was devastated. I asked him over and over if he was sure and he told me he was 98% certain. Just thinking about it made my heart break all over again and yet I couldn't help but feel glad that I didn't tell Jake about Annalise. That was just one less complicated thing I had to deal with I supposed.

The morning sun filtered through the semi dusty windows and the only company I had to put up with were the nurses that came in to take my blood pressure every two hours. Around quarter to eight I heard muffled arguments outside the room and I just couldn't find it in me to care so I went back to counting tiles on the ceiling.

Suddenly he door burst open and my head snapped towards it. I stifled a gasp when I saw Jake standing there with a mixture of emotions spread across his face. He looked a mess. A sexy mess, but a mess nonetheless. He strode over to me and before I had the time to squeak 'Jake!' his lips were on mine. His lips were hard and demanding and I could sense a hidden pain behind his sudden intrusion. By the time our kiss broke I was gasping for air.

Jake leaned forward and pressed his forehead to mine. "Why didn't you tell me?" his voice broke quietly.

I stiffened. "Tell you what?"

He moved back slightly and cupped my cheek with his big roughened hands. "That you were carrying my baby. I would've been there for you through everything Sasha"

And that was all it took. The walls I put up to my grief broke like an overflowing dam and I began crying harder than ever. Jake knew I was pregnant, and he would've been supportive of me. My body was trembling and Jake sat on the bed the whole time just holding me and shedding a few tears as well.

Hours passed and Jake never left my side. He was my solid rock of strength and it only made me fall in love with him more and more. He was my perfect man and because of my experiment I couldn't be with him. I hated myself. I lost my baby and I couldn't be with Jake. Being with him would only ever be beautiful memories.

Finally I was discharged and while we walked out to the car I noticed the nurses and Jake having some sort of stare down. "What's that all about?" I nodded my chin towards them.

"I may have had a few words to say to them this morning when they refused to let me in to see you before eight o'clock. I don't think they like me very much"

"Sasha! Oh my God!" I was enveloped in a tight suffocating hug by Jenna when Jake opened the door of my apartment. "The baby..."

"I guess it wasn't the right time for me..." I whispered.

"Oh Sasha, I'm so sorry" she consoled me as she hugged me again.

Jenna and Jake stayed until night just keeping me company. I was thoroughly grateful for their company and support but I was getting tired and needed time alone. I began yawning loudly and Jenna seemed to pick up on my subtle hints.

"Well, I guess I better be off. If you ever need anything Sash I'm just a call away okay?" she called out before letting herself out.

"Come on, bed time" Jake said pushing me to my bedroom. I assumed he would turn off my lights before leaving but I was surprised when I finished changing into a baggy shirt and turned around to se him walking in behind me and taking his shirt off.

"Jake! What are you doing?" I squeaked.

"Going to bed. Don't worry Sasha, it's nothing sexual" he replied before pulling me to the bed with him. "I just want to make sure you're not alone, especially at a time like this"

I let him tuck me in before sliding under the covers next to me and I sighed in bliss when he pulled me into his arms to spoon me. I could feel his lips brushing against my hair and it was like I was back home when I was in his arms like this.

"Thank you" I whispered. I hoped he realised that I was saying thank you for more than just being here today.

"Sasha... I'll be here for you whenever you need me. I can see how you're still trying to be strong in front of me but you don't need to. I want to be the one to be strong for you" he paused to kiss my hair again before continuing. "Why didn't you tell me when you found out?"

I knew he would want to know and I was hoping he wouldn't ask. "I was scared. I offered you no strings attached sex Jake. How could I go running back when I'd already left the country to say that I was pregnant? I thought you would have thought I was trying to worm myself back into your life or something"

Silence followed before he turned me around to face him. "I wouldn't have cared if you told me over the phone Sasha. I would have flown to the other side of the world to be there for you" He swiped his thumb below my eye catching the tears that fell. "No more tears... please."

We fell asleep wrapped tightly around each other and I dreamt of the times we had together on our island paradise.

I woke to my phone ringing in the morning and quickly detangled myself from Jake's warm body to answer it without waking him. "Hello?" I answered the private number.

"Good morning, my name is Mary from the Pindaro Hospital. Is this Sasha Montgomery?" a woman's voice spoke.

"Uh, yes it is. What can I do for you Mary?" I answered.

"Well Sasha, I'm the head early pregnancy nurse here at Pindaro Hospital and I was informed that you stayed here overnight and were admitted through emergency for a miscarriage?" she asked, though it was more of a statement.

"Yes, that's correct"

"Ok, well I'm calling just to see how your pain and bleeding is"

"I'm not in any pain actually. It pretty much subsided when I was in emergency and my bleeding is pretty much spotting" I explained.

"Hmm... I see. Well Sasha, I was going over your blood work and I'm not entirely sure that you did have a miscarriage. Usually the pain and bleeding should last longer than what you experienced. There's a spare spot for an ultrasound in two hours if you would like?"

Hope bloomed within me. Could it really be true? Could my little Annalise be alive? I immediately jumped at the chance. "Yes! YES! Definitely!" I practically screamed.

Mary laughed lightly on the phone, "No problem. Now I would suggest going to the bathroom now and drinking at least a litre of water. Do not empty your bladder until after the ultrasound" I nodded even though she couldn't see me and after a few more instructions I hung up the phone and ran to the bathroom.

Jakes' POV

I reached over to hug Sasha closer to me and frowned when there was nothing but empty cold space. I opened my eyes and saw the bathroom door closed and heard the shower running. The water shut off and Sasha came bursting through the door followed by hot steam and immediately began rifling through her closet.

"Well good morning Sasha" I croaked.

"Get dressed Jake!" she shouted in response. I raised an eyebrow and slipped out of her bed to walk behind her.

"Hey, are you okay?" I said kissing her shoulder.

"More than okay Jake! I'm ecstatic!" she beamed. For a moment my breath was caught in my throat at her beautiful smile but then confusion set in at her words.

"May I ask why?"

"Jake, I got a call from the early pregnancy nurse and she doesn't think I had a miscarriage! I have an ultrasound at ten o'clock so let's go, let's go, let's go!"

She seemed so happy and hopeful that I didn't have it in me to squash the fact that the doctor had said he was 98% certain she'd miscarried. I followed suite though and readied myself for her ultrasound, even though I wasn't as hopeful as she was.

"Stop bouncing Sasha, we'll be in in a second" I laughed holding her knees down.

"I really need to pee Jake! You don't understand how much water I drank!" she snapped.

"So why don't you go to the bathroom?" I asked scrunching my face in confusion. It was the most obvious action right?

"Because it helps with the ultrasound. The emergency doctor did the ultrasound on me to check if the baby was there but I'd gone to the bathroom earlier so it would've been harder to see!"

Ooh... that made sense, I suppose.

Soon enough we were greeted by a friendly looking lady and in no time Sasha was lying back on a bed getting clear gel squirted onto her belly.

No one spoke as the lady worked and the suspense was killing me. I looked down at Sasha and saw she was craning her neck to look at the screen, so I held her hand and offered her a smile.

"Okay..." the lady said stretching out the word. She turned the screen around and pointed at it. "Here is your little girl, completely safe and sound in your belly"

I swear a tumbleweed blew past in my head accompanied by chirping crickets.

A baby girl...!

"Oh my God! Annalise is still alive!" Sasha squealed.

"You see this darker part close to the baby? That was the area that bled out, so it was close but it didn't affect your little bub" the lady smiled.

"Argh! That emergency doctor told me he was 98% certain I'd miscarried!" Sasha growled.

"What?! You wouldn't happen to know his name would you? I will hit him!" the lady frowned. Sasha and the ultrasound lady conversed while Sasha cleaned up and I just sat there in shock.

Sasha is still pregnant.

With my baby.

With my baby girl.

Annalise.

16

Epilogue

S asha's POV

I groaned as I rolled over in bed for the third time tonight. This incessant need to go to the bathroom every few hours was extremely tiring. It was still dark outside and I didn't bother to look at the clock as I literally rolled myself off the bed to my feet and began trudging towards the toilet.

I was now 35 weeks pregnant and well into my third trimester, however no matter how many times I felt the calling, I never got used to running back and forwards to the bathroom. I was practically wearing down the carpet.

After I relieved myself I saw the numbers on the clock read 4.30am. I sighed and wondered if it was worth going back to bed. Instead I walked down the hallway to the bedroom next door and pushed it open. I was so excited to have it finally completed. Jake had been adamant about buying everything and anything for Annalise and the whole room pretty much consisted of a cot and about a million boxes and bags.

Annalise squirmed inside of me and I rubbed my swollen belly subconsciously. She was growing bigger and now had little room for those big kicks and now would just wriggle around having fun pushing against my bladder.

"Are you done with your acrobatics baby girl?" I spoke to her as I skimmed my fingers over the swell of my stomach. I was answered by her elbow, or knee, rubbing down the front of my tummy and I smiled. "Life's never lonely with you is it sweety?" I chuckled.

I yawned wide and headed back to my cold bed tossing the sheets over me. Today was Saturday and with nothing to fill my day ahead I decided to drive over to Jenna's house for some quality time with her.

"WHAT ARE YOU DOING HERE?!" I was greeted by a wide-eyed Jenna as she opened the front door of her house.

"Uh... hello to you too Jen. I'm visiting... I'm not disturbing you am I?" I asked nervously. I never usually called or gave notice when I would visit her on the weekend but this time it seemed like I was a little unwelcomed.

She sighed heavily and rolled her eyes. "No, come on in"

She turned to walk inside and I followed her shutting the oak door. As I continued down the hallway to her lounge I gasped. There were literally hundreds of pink and white balloons littering the floor and a mess of streamers of the same colours being strung across the walls.

"What's going on?" I asked curiously.

"Well! It was SUPPOSED to be your surprise baby shower seeing as you've been too lazy to throw one yourself but it seems like you got your surprise a little earlier than expected" Jenna explained.

"No way!" I squealed as a huge smile painted its way across my face. "Jenna you are absolutely the BEST friend anyone could have!"

I hugged her tightly which earned me a laugh and a tight embrace back. We walked further into her house to her kitchen and I took a seat on one of her bar stools as she made herself coffee.

"Coffee?" she offered.

"I don't think I can drink coffee remember?" I replied pointing at my belly.

"Oh right!" She laughed, "Water then?" I nodded and we chatted until her coffee was finished.

"Can I help with anything?" I asked. There were a few people around the house decorating and cleaning, because let's face it... who has a spotless house 24/7 when no one is around.

"Uh... well since you crashed your own surprise I guess you can watch the food in case they burn" she nodded towards the kitchen again.

I nodded and set up the food as well as cleaned a bit. It was already eleven and apparently the baby shower started at one-thirty. I was considering going to the bathroom again and wondered if I could just finish baking the pasta before I went when I started to feel something drip between my legs.

"Oh shoot" I mumbled when I began to walk to the toilet. I guess being pregnant and having a wriggling baby against my bladder didn't help with my muscles down there. I did my business and was silently thanking myself for wearing a long maxi dress.

I washed up and walked back out when I thought back to what happened. I couldn't have...? No. Not possible. I was only 35 weeks... I just stood in the hallway thinking hard, contemplating whether or not I should tell Jenna my thoughts. Just at that moment Jenna walked into the hallway holding a bag full of streamers.

"Hey Sasha, you alright? You look like you're thinking a little hard there" she joked.

"I... THINK...my water broke..." I said softly.

Jenna made a confused face before moving in closer, "Sorry I don't think I heard you properly. What did you say?"

I cleared my throat and spoke a little louder, "I said I THINK my water broke"

"What!"

Jenna's face was a mix of shock and excitement but I barely got to glance at her before I felt a strong dripping sensation down my legs. I sprinted as fast as my pregnant body could allow and as I sat on the toilet my mind was screaming 'YES YOUR WATER FREAKING BROKE!'

Jenna began rapping against the door, "Sasha are you okay? Are you sure your water broke?"

"Yep!" I replied dragging out the 'y'.

We walked back to the kitchen and Jenna was a mess! "Okay! You need to sit down and call Jake! He said he'd be at the office before he was supposed to pick you up because he had an important meeting. So you call him and I'll call the hospital! Actually no! You walk around a little while calling him, that's supposed to help quicken the labour!"

Honestly, if I hadn't started to have stronger contractions I'd be laughing at her frenzied state. I'd begun having pretty strong Braxton Hicks when I started my third trimester so I thought that's what these were last night but I guessed wrong.

I walked back and forth while Jake's phone continued to ring. He wouldn't pick up the phone and soon enough I was feeling a mood swing hit me. I'd gotten pretty good at sensing when they were going to change.

"Sasha, I'm taking you to the hospital now. I'll just have someone call everyone to say that you're in labour and the baby shower's cancelled" Jenna called out to me. I nodded but was in no rush. I'd been timing my contractions and I was nowhere near five minutes apart.

I'd probably tried ringing Jake literally thirty times with no answer so I turned to texting him instead.

'Why the FUCK aren't you picking up your phone?! My water broke! Jenna is taking me to the hospital now! Meet me there!'

Okay... so maybe that was a little harsh but that should get him moving pretty quickly.

I was rushed into the car and luckily for us the hospital was only ten minutes away. My stomach tightened with every contraction and I grimaced as I checked my watch. They'd been coming and going at such different times that I wondered how long my labour would end up being! Technically I'm not supposed to go there until they're five minutes apart right?

My phone buzzed in my hand and I sighed in relief when I saw Jake's number flashing.

"Hell-"

"SASHA ARE YOU ALRIGHT! WHERE ARE YOU? I'M AL-READY AT THE HOSPITAL BUT I CAN'T SEE YOU!"

"Geez, calm down you crazy person. I'm fine! I'm still in the car and-" I paused as I clutched at my stomach and moaned as another contraction wracked my body, "we're almost there"

We reached the hospital and Jake was pacing out the front. Once he turned and saw Jenna's car he ran towards us and practically carried me up to the labour ward. I was put into a bed and the whole time I didn't have a contraction. I was checked to see how far along I was into labour and according to the midwife I'd only broken my water and wasn't even dilated.

"Looks, like you'll be here for a while Sasha" she joked as she checked my monitor.

My contractions were still random but were becoming much, much more strong. Each one would spread a wave of pain from my lower back around to my front and my immediate reaction was to stop breathing.

"Sorry, love but the pain will get worse" I was told by a nurse when I asked how long it was between contractions. Not even close to five minutes yet!

Within minutes the waves of pain were non-stop. There was no pause or gap for me to gasp for air or relax my body from its cramped position and it was almost impossible for me to even roll to my side to ease some of the pain. Oh God! Why wasn't it stopping! I began to cry and grit my teeth.

"Oh my God! It cannot possibly get worse than this!!! It's only been fifteen minutes!" I cried.

The midwife made a concerned face, "Hmm, I'll just check and see how dilated you are and maybe we can see why you're in so much pain okay?" She lifted the sheets up and gasped, "Oh! Sasha your baby's head is here! You're going to need to push on the next contraction!"

I groaned in pain as my body heated up and sweat dampened my body. No fucking wonder it hurt so much!

"I'm here Sasha! I'm here. Just breathe... breathe" Jake cooed into my ear while trying not grimace at the iron hold I had on his hand.

"No! YOU breathe! I swear to God Jake if you say 'breathe' one more time I will RIP your voice box out from your fucking throat!" I growled at him.

"And I'd still be here even if you did Sash" he countered.

"The head's out, just one more push!" the midwife called out.

I screamed louder than I'd ever screamed before as I used all my energy in my body to push my daughter out, and if Jenna or Jake cried out in pain from me squeezing their hands then I couldn't hear them.

My body dropped from the arch I'd somehow pushed myself into and I gasped for air like the world was running out of it. My body was tingling and my throat was raw.

The next thing I knew I could hear Jenna crying and laughing while Jake's smell enveloped me as he leaned close to my ear, "She's beautiful Sasha. Thank you! Thank you for making me the happiest father in the world!" I could hear the hitch in his voice as he spoke and knew a tear or two were making their way down his chiselled face.

"Is-is she okay?" I stammered as I fought myself to stay awake.

"Perfect. Absolutely perfect Sasha! She cried as loud as you screamed as soon as she was out" he answered with pride in his voice.

It was seconds before the midwife approached me with a tiny pink bundle. "Would you like to hold your daughter, Sasha?" she asked rhetorically with a large smile.

"Definitely!" I nodded eagerly. After what seemed like way too long the warm blankets were placed into my awaiting arms and, for the first time, I peeked at the most perfect little face.

Her face was pink and her eyes were a little swollen. Her tiny nose took quick breaths and exhaled through the most adorable pink lips. Her head was covered by the blankets but from what I could see she had a little tuff of dark, fine hair. She was complete perfection. My eyes were glued to her face and I waited for every breath and every little twitch her face made.

It was hard, but I ripped my eyes from my daughter and looked at Jake, "Would you like to hold her?" I asked, but winced when the words hurt my throat. It literally felt like my throat had been slashed from all my screaming.

It looked like Jake was trying to talk, but couldn't, so he nodded instead. I turned slowly and slid my little bundle of pure perfection into his big, warm arms. When he stood up I swear I lost my breath. Jake holding our daughter in his arms was a beautiful sight. Annalise was so small and innocent and completely fragile while Jake was big, strong and powerful yet it looked 100% natural for him to be carrying her.

"Hi Annalise" he whispered with his head bent low almost touching hers, "I'm your daddy"

The moment he closed his eyes and kissed Annalise's forehead I knew I was a goner. How could I possibly live without this man in me and my daughter's life?